The Author

DAVID ADAMS RICHARDS was born in Newcastle, New Brunswick, in 1950. After attending St. Thomas University in Fredericton for three years, he turned his fulltime attention to writing. From 1983 to 1987 he was writer-in-residence at the University of New Brunswick, later accepting similar positions, for shorter periods of time, at other universities.

Richards creates his fictional universe out of his native Miramichi River Valley in northern New Brunswick. His characters, usually of the working class, struggle to preserve their moral courage and their dignity in a world increasingly displaced by economic and social changes. Their sometimes violent lives hide, though never completely, the generosity, tenderness, and love in their many relationships.

David Adams Richards lives in Toronto, Ontario.

THE NEW CANADIAN LIBRARY

General Editor: David Staines

David Adams Richards

EVENING SNOW WILL BRING SUCH PEACE

Afterword by Wayne Johnston

M&S

The following dedication appeared in the original edition:

For all those who stand beside those who stand alone
this book is dedicated.

Copyright © 1990 by David Adams Richards
Afterword copyright © 2003 by Wayne Johnston

This book was first published by McClelland & Stewart in 1990
New Canadian Library edition 2003

National Library of Canada Cataloguing in Publication

Richards, David Adams, 1950-
Evening snow will bring such peace / David Adams Richards ;
with an afterword by Wayne Johnston.

(New Canadian library)
ISBN 0-7710-3485-7

I. Title. II. Series.

PS8585.I17E9 2003   C813'.54   C2003-901761-3
PR9199.3.R465E9 2003

We acknowledge the financial support of the Government of Canada
through the Book Publishing Industry Development Program and that of
the Government of Ontario through the Ontario Media Development
Corporation's Ontario Book Initiative. We further acknowledge the
support of the Canada Council for the Arts and the Ontario Arts Council
for our publishing program.

Typesetting by M&S, Toronto
Printed and bound in Canada

McClelland & Stewart Ltd.
The Canadian Publishers
481 University Avenue
Toronto, Ontario
M5G 2E9
www.mcclelland.com/NCL

1 2 3 4 5   07 06 05 04 03

And those who longest should have met
Are safe in each other's arms not too late.
Today the forsaken one of the fold is brought home –

The tortured shall no longer know alarm

– Malcolm Lowry

But take heed lest by any means this liberty of yours become a
stumblingblock to them that are weak.

– Paul – 1 Cor. 8:9.

I

1

Ivan Basterache had been married twenty months. But now he and Cindi were separated. The trouble had started because Ivan's father had borrowed a thousand dollars from Vera, his next-door neighbour, and then had asked Ivan to intercede. So Ivan had taken Cindi's money to pay the debt. A fight followed and chairs were broken, and the very money was torn to shreds. The RCMP had to come because of the shotgun, and Cindi ran outside in her underwear and went to Ruby Madgill's.

Ivan drove into town a few days later. He left the car and walked along the street, passed the old red-brick opera house, and moved along with his hands in his pockets.

He found himself in the heart of town without realizing where he was. He went into the park and sat on a bench just in front of the bust of Lord Beaverbrook. Then after lighting a cigarette he got up and moved again. He had no idea where he was going, and seemed to be moving in circles.

Of course you don't always know where you are going – but for some reason all movements happen because they were meant to.

Therefore he found himself at Ralphie Pillar's shop at noon hour. Ralphie was Vera's brother.

The shop, in the back part of an empty cafeteria on a side street above the post office, was small and dark. A blind was drawn down over the white radiator that sat below the window and collected dust. There was an airplane engine against one wall, and a telescope on the table near the door. The whole place was cluttered with leftover parts of engines and typewriters, with coins and clocks – the clocks all ticking, and all telling a different time – but with no Paris, Vienna, or Moscow labelled beneath them. Where Ralphie had acquired all of this stuff Ivan did not know.

Ivan walked right up to him, with a boldness he always had, his eyes very bright and yet always a little detached from the moment; the eyes, in fact, of a person who has survived and lived by himself, without much help in early youth from anyone – neither mother nor father.

The first time that Ralphie had seen him Ivan had been standing alone, in the snow, wearing a thin jacket, on Christmas night in 1972. Ralphie and his girlfriend, Adele Walsh, passed him by – the air was clear, they had come from church, and they were on their way to the apartment. And Ralphie was singing. Ivan, who knew Adele just slightly, began smiling in great satisfaction, as if he had been standing alone in the middle of the street just to hear that song, and then he began to trek through the light snow beside them, now and then dropping back when they kissed, and then hurrying on again to catch up. Every time

Ralphie looked at him, he smiled and nodded in the exact same manner.

Finally, he waited outside while Ralphie climbed the stairs to the apartment, suddenly realizing that he hadn't the key. Ivan looked up at him from the doorway, the air seeming to lay against him in a perennial sort of winter delight, and glittering snow fell on his hat.

"Well – this looks like a break-in scrape," Ivan said.

"It doesn't matter," Ralphie said, smiling in a worried way.

"You want to show young Delly" – he was six months older than Adele – "yer apartment, then just wait."

It was dark and cold, and he was gone. But now and again Ralphie could hear a noise, just slightly it shuddered through the dark empty winter night, snow falling away, and the kicking of a boot.

Then the door opened and Ivan looked out at them and said:

"It's not too bad a place at all – I'd put a waterbed in her though."

That was how Ralphie had come to know Ivan Basterache six years ago, and how Ivan had come to know him.

Now Ralphie was stooped over, replacing a flywheel on a machine. It was a tiny little flywheel, and he worked for some time without knowing Ivan was there.

One of his problems – besides his tremendous fallibility of tinkering endlessly at small jobs – was his refusal to collect on bills.

Ralphie and Adele, now married, were living with his mother Thelma, because his mother wanted him near her, and because he made very little money in his shop, which Thelma was continually bringing up to him and telling him he should go back to university.

Everything about Ralphie, from his cowboy boots, caked in mud, to his thin shirt covering an equally thin body, and his large head, with his broad white forehead, was somehow, to Ivan, innocent. That is the only word he could think of, and he didn't know why.

"Well, I suppose you heard," Ivan said, in sort of half disgust, not at all because he felt disgust or anything else, he was too upset to feel this, but because this was the attitude he hoped would betray nothing.

Ralphie turned about, looked at him, and blushed.

Of course, everyone had heard. Ivan's horseplay would make most men turn pale, and everyone had been waiting for the marriage to fall apart.

"Well, I want a divorce is what I want," Ivan said, without knowing a minute before that he would ever say anything like this. "I want to get it over with," he said.

Ralphie was trying to keep his eyes averted but could not. And suddenly he broke out grinning from ear to ear.

"A divorce," Ralphie said.

"A divorce – divorce – divorce," Ivan said furiously.

He said this with a sort of fierce judgement of his own stupidity.

"Anyway," he said, still not sure why he was saying it, "it's best – she can find a lot bettern me."

"Oh, who says?" Ralphie said.

"Everyone wants me to say that, and won't be satisfied until it is said," Ivan said heatedly, as if Ralphie suddenly had become another enemy. "And anyway," he said, "who would want to put up with me?" He sniffed, suddenly satisfied with this statement. "And

6

besides, I'll be much more happier." Then he added, "Look, Ralphie, I didn't hit her as they say – well, not as they say – she took a seizure. We were having a big fight, she took a seizure and fell flat on her fuckin knob –"

"I didn't say you did," Ralphie said.

Ralphie was silent.

"Do you think I should see a lawyer?" he said.

"No," Ralphie said.

"I want to know if I need a divorce in this here racket and yer my friend," Ivan said.

"Why don't you go down and talk to Cindi about it."

"If I ever see her again, I'll kill her," Ivan said matter-of-factly. "So I better not. She's been on this big drunk – and she's not taking her medicine either – so don't let her kid you if she says she's been taking her medicine."

He said this as if Cindi not taking her medicine proved conclusively that he was in the right.

"I don't want to get involved anyways," Ralphie said.

Ivan shoved his hands in his pockets and nodded. "Oh."

"Well – you know what I mean."

Ivan nodded once more and shrugged.

"I don't even know what lawyer to go to," Ivan said, smiling guiltily. "What lawyer should I go to, Ralphie?"

"Well, there are lots of good lawyers," Ralphie said.

Ivan scratched his head. His hair was curly and short, his eyes bright.

"If I go to any lawyer – they'll say what were you doing, and I'll say we were having this big fight over her money, and I had the shotgun out and she took a seizure. That don't sound very good."

Ralphie looked up at him and could not help smiling.

"But except when I threw spaghetti over her head – I didn't touch her," Ivan said. "There, I told you about the spaghetti – that's it."

Ralphie said nothing.

"That might have brought on the seizure, but she's not taking her medicine – and don't you think she is," he said, pointing his finger at nothing in particular.

Ivan then went walking about the shop, picking things up and putting them back down.

"I come home – there she is. 'Look, you son of a bitch,' I said, 'Dad's in another big scrape, so where's that money?' And she runs to get it for me – and she had this apron on with deer on the pockets, and those big Sasquatch slippers on her feet, and she runs to get the money – and then when I see her sitting on the couch with the box and counting – and when she counts she moves her lips. Then she made a mistake."

"A mistake?"

"She got to a hundred and seventy dollars and had to start all over. I yelled, 'Yer at 170 – you dumb quiff – count!' And she said, '170?' and I saw her get scared. She said, '170–160–164.' Then I picked the money up and tore it in pieces, and threw it across the room. 'Fuck the money,' I said. 'And the hell with Dad – let him pay his own debts for once.' And then she did what she always did, she folded her arms and looked at her shoes – and started counting to ten. And you know why she was counting to ten? Because she got mixed up. It was me who was supposed to count to ten. I had told her that if I ever got angry – and she's scared of my temper – I would count to ten.

"'Why are you counting to ten?' I yelled. She wouldn't answer. 'WHY IN FUCK ARE YOU COUNTING TO TEN?' She wouldn't answer. Finally she said, 'I'm angry so I'm counting to ten – so there.' The poor little thing, as if 'so there' was going to solve everything in the world forever."

"I'm sorry that the money for Vera caused everything," Ralphie said.

"You don't understand! *That's* not the problem, Ralphie. I had to help out my dad. And it was no big deal – I mean, it was my Heath Steele Mine money anyway. But then I took the money and I tore it up. Why did I do that?"

"I don't know," Ralphie answered.

"Why did I do that – why did I tear the money up?" They were silent.

"Then after a while, she got up off the couch – I'm sitting in the kitchen – and she went over to the money and got on her hands and knees and started to tape it up. That's when I went crazy – told her not to touch it – and things happened. She went running outside – it was cold too – I got the shotgun –"

Then, as if he had completely forgotten about his own problems, he asked Ralphie how his mother was, and if she still had pains in her left hand – something which she had seven months ago, and which Ralphie had forgotten completely about.

Then he asked Ralphie about the things he was doing civically. That is, Ralphie had joined the Kinsmen and believed they were the best and most responsible civic organization in town, simply because he was sure he was supposed to feel this way.

His mother, Thelma, had wanted him to be active about town, and so hung his older sister, Vera, over his head – that is, all as Thelma would have to say is: "Oh yes – I have Vera – now I have you!"

And all as Adele had to say was: "I have no friends and I never get anywhere – and I'm nothin to no one in this here life – I mayswell have my tubes tied in a granny knot or even be dead." So he joined the Kinsmen and the Toastmasters, and would work fourteen to sixteen hours a day.

They had a child when Adele was just a teenager, and they had given that child up to Ralphie's childless aunt and uncle, Olive and Gerald Dressard. Though they knew where it was, they decided it would be best not to see it, and though they said it was for the best (because his mother and his sister had both told them that it was), they worried about it and wondered what it was doing at any given moment. And sometimes when Adele heard Thelma talking about children, and how these little children were victims and should not be born – except maybe every once in a while, but not all the time, like rabbits – Adele would take it as a direct assault upon herself.

Other than that they never spoke of their child. But sometimes Thelma would become fond of saying: "Oh, there's lots of time for you two to have children!" Or: "I can't wait to have a grandchild – and now Vera is finally pregnant. You two just don't know how important grandchildren are."

And it was not that Thelma had forgotten, sometimes she was piously delighted at the instant she said it.

At these times Adele would stare straight ahead, and her eyes would become fixed on something.

Adele, as yet, wasn't spoken of as being a part of

10

the family. She looked, to others, even walking with them to church, to be a sort of an appendage, a hanger-on.

It was a peculiar situation. She and Ralphie lived with Thelma because Thelma insisted – had pleaded that they do – and yet, since they did, neither of them were allowed to forget it. Sometimes Adele would pack her old brown suitcase and haul it down the long white-carpeted staircase (much like she had packed her overnight bag in 1973, the time she ran away from home) and, sitting in the den staring out the window at the oxidized maple leaves blowing across the large circular driveway, she would start to cry.

Thelma would then bring her daughter Vera into it, ask her opinion – as an older woman will, at times, ingratiate herself to the opinions of a younger one – to prove to others that she, too, can agree with such "morally challenging" opinions. Vera always said that Adele and Ralphie were not suited because of "*class* differences."

These were the things that had been on Ralphie's mind when Ivan came into the office.

Now Ivan patiently waited in the swivel chair by the phone. He was reflecting that Cindi might phone Ralphie to ask where he was – and that everything might solve itself.

Just then the telephone did ring. Ivan gave a start, stood up and went to the door, turned about, and looked at the phone again. He was in a state that so many people get into when they have their minds set on something terrible happening. He had trained his mind for the inevitable to happen, and now he perversely desired it to happen.

Ralphie picked up the phone. In an instant Ivan knew (and reflecting later, he knew this by the way the telephone rang) that it wasn't Cindi.

"I knew she wouldn't call," Ivan said when Ralphie hung up, and then he smiled.

And instead of waiting one more second, he went out into the street, cursing raw and bare words, leaving the door bang open behind him.

"Wait," Ralphie said, "wait – we'll phone her. . . . "

❖ ❖ ❖

Ivan continued to stay out behind the apartment building in the woods for a number of days. It was April and the woods were very damp. But he was able to make out all right. It wasn't the best of situations.

He could see Ruby and Cindi. On a warm day they would barbecue out on the patio. He moved back and forth in the woods, along well-worn deer trails and back pastures that were still snowpacked.

He knew that Ruby didn't like him. He didn't like her either – he thought she was spoiled. But that Ruby did not like him caused consternation now. He pretended, if only to himself, as he walked through the woods, that he didn't know why she didn't like him. But that was not quite the truth. The truth was more subtle. Ivan understood it only in a very shadowy way when he came up against it, and until now he had never had any need to face it. Ruby had always considered him puritanical, always trying to ruin either her or Cindi's fun. Ivan, she supposed, did not have any idea of fun. Ivan had always seen that in her face when she spoke to him. And perhaps she was right about him. She had a beautiful face, too, a tiny stud ring in her nose, and her eyes as sharp as blue splinters. But he would pass her by morosely. She would talk loudly in his presence, telling Cindi about things they should do, things Ivan had no interest in.

Ivan saw in these few days that Ruby wished for Cindi to once again have this fun, to bring her into it, in a manner which would seem once and for all to exclude him. For if he advanced on them to stop it, it would only be proof of the puritanical, brutal strain Ruby was now convincing herself and Cindi that he had.

He did not know that people used words like shotgun blasts in the dark.

Once, a long time ago, Ivan went down to Vera and Nevin's place to deliver a parcel for Ralphie. Vera, this first time they met, hearing that this young, jean-jacketed youth with dark lively eyes and a pug nose, and large hardened hands with tattoos on his knuckles, was about to be married, took him aside. And, as if she were being watched by the obscure matron of those ethics Ivan knew nothing about, Vera spoke reverently to him abut the position of women in society today. He caught only that glimpse of the hidden world where certain ethics were at war, which he knew, or Cindi knew, nothing about.

He could remember of that day the smell of the fine linen in her hand as she folded it against her stomach as she spoke, and this, along with her quiet, measured voice, left with him the idea of sincerity, which very few other people had ever done. This and the way her husband Nevin moved back and forth, trying not to intrude – much like a brother would not intrude

13

upon a priest giving a lecture to an altar boy about the moral danger of masturbation – gave him a sense that they felt their duty was to instruct. He had no real idea of why.

He had a better idea of the motives of the police. But they had no idea about him, or the shotgun. The reason he had the shotgun out was to destroy the large oak cabinet in the living room. Since his father had continually for the last twenty months helped himself in one way or the other to those meagre savings of his and Cindi's, Ivan, in taking his anger out on the oak cabinet, their favourite piece of furniture, believed he was reducing everything to its logical conclusion.

He tore the money up for a more obscure reason – but a reason the police would not consider. Nor would any legislative assembly, speaking, as they often do today, on family violence. Ivan could not stand that he had started this argument over something so shallow as money. It was better to be rid of it, tear it to shreds.

Yet he was still resolved to pay Vera and Nevin back.

Everything was suddenly looked at, not in this light, such as it was, but in the shadows he had been sometimes shown by the more obscure motives of others. He did not understand them as well as he should have, he was too certain of life to be bothered by them; he only knew that they were there.

The police had not charged him as yet, so it was a matter that was too insignificant for them to hurry over. This also gave him a sense of disquiet. He felt by this almost made light of.

Finally, after five days, Ivan went back to the apartment and packed his clothes, took his buck knife and rifle, and moved onto his grandfather's old lobster boat.

"So you are leaving her," someone said.

"She has left me also," he replied.

✛   ✛   ✛

Living together and married, their life was, for that short time, never boring.

In the winter Ivan would get home after dark. Then, after supper, he would go out and take long walks up behind the high line – where Adele's father, Joe Walsh, had his camp, or in the fall he would take a bucket of apples and put them out at the edge of a field, or he would put a salt-lick down somewhere, or have his back pockets filled with carrots or lettuce.

Once he said: "Well, Cindi, there's a dry doe coming out behind Ruby's paddock in the morning – and that little buck is there as well – but I don't think he's going to last too long with the poachers about." It made no difference to Ivan that he was a poacher himself. "I have to work tomorrow, so I want you to take a walk, and take that road up to the left of the high line behind there, into Joe Walsh's – Joe knows me – I'm a big friend of his, so he won't mind. And if he does mind, too bad about him."

"And what am I spose to do, Ivan?"

"I'll tell you what yer spose to do," Ivan said, as if he just this moment thought of it. "You have to see if the deer are crossing the road. Just check for signs up to the big puddle – or," he said, brightening up again, as if he just thought of this as well, and now it had become indispensable to his train of thought, "you could take my waders and put them on – of course you'd look like Popeye's son Sweetpea in them – and try not to get stuck in the middle of the puddle or you'll get all puddled up and drown or something – and watch out for moose. On your left on the other side is a little path which goes down to Joe's camp at Brookwall. Better yet," he said, brightening up once more, "take a barrel of apples – as many as you can – saddle Troy, tickle the back part of his mouth to get the bit in, and take those bunch of apples I got down there by the laundry basket, just hang a bucket of them off the horn – or, better yet, tie the bucket to the horn and then through the back split where the show girth is spose to go – so then you won't have to worry about it –"

"The show what?" Cindi said, blinking at him and moving her knees together and the toes of her sneakers so that they touched one another.

"Show girth," Ivan said lackadaisically. "And make sure you watch all the time, for there might be someone who mistakes you for a moose and shoots you – we can never be sure who's out there in the woods with a rifle. It's usually Dad. But don't be scared of them – better yet, you may as well take the rifle – not my .306, because it'll knock your shoulder off – take the .30-30."

"Which one is which?"

"I'm not going to answer that because I've told you a thousand times which is which – and I'll probably never be able to tell you – you'll just have to figure it out sooner or later, but I'll give you just a small hint – it's that one right there." He pointed. "You used it last summer when we went target practising – dontcha remember?"

Cindi nodded and tapped her sneakers together.

They were silent for quite some time.

Then Ivan, sitting at the small round table with the flowered plastic table mats, noticed Cindi talking to herself.

"What?"

"I'm just trying to remember all you told me to do."

"Well never mind – just do what you can remember, when you remember to do it."

Then the telephone rang and Ivan answered it and yelled: "What's goin on! Oh hello, Doris – you old dog. How's your mustn't-touch-it? What? No problem – if I can get the car started – ya, ya, ya – "

Then he hung the receiver up gently, mused over something, and put on his boots, untied. His eyes looked both gentle and wild, and his tattooed hands were scarred from climbing trees to throw raccoons to the ground. The raccoons would tear at his hands as he threw them out of the trees, and when they landed on the ground they would all run away. "Don't tree them if you can't handle them," Ivan yelled, swaying from the top limb, forty feet in the air.

Then he went over to Doris's to tear down a nest the wasps had built just above her porch. When he came back he gave sugar lumps to the horses – being extra nice to Troy, and Ruby's horse, Tantramar.

When he got back into the house, he said to Cindi: "She yelled at me not to drop the nest, so here I go and get stung by fifty of them or maybe a hundred." He lowered his shirt collar to show the welts on his neck. For a moment he seemed to reflect on this.

"I'll put some ice on those," Cindi said.

"Yes, ice me down for Christ's sake – or I'll go into shock or something. That's the last wasp nest I'll ever take down from her porch."

He folded his arms resolutely and tapped his feet.

"That don't matter for poor old Doris," he reflected, smiling, and lighting a cigarette quickly, as if to hide this tender reflection.

The next morning Cindi tried to think of all the things he had told her, and, going out to the edge of the paddock, she shifted the bucket of apples from one arm to the other, and, wearing a pair of huge waders that were tied about her neck, she stared gloomily off into the distant high line. And after walking twenty yards or so, feeling the wind at her back, blowing against the long, cold furrows of a muddy field, with the sun lukewarm in the greying sky, she began to back up again. Little by little, she backed up until she reached the spot where she had been. Then with fierce resolution she turned and walked back to the apartment.

"What did you manage to do?" Ivan asked at supper that evening.

"I managed to get your waders on – but I had to tie them up with that friggin old garter belt that was left down in the basement – by that woman."

"That's the very best – did you take the apples?"

"I took some apples, and I went out to the field –"

"That's the very best – you saddle Troy?"

"No, I didn't think of it."

"No, that was a bad idea. Thought of that at work and came to the decision that it was a bad idea anyways –"

"So anyways, I didn't take the rifle because you have two kinds of bullets –"

"Ya – that's right, as I was thinking I wouldn't want you to blow your head off anyways. So did you see if they were crossing the road?"

"I didn't see them on the road."

"Where did you put the apples?"

"Pardon?"

"The apples?"

"Well, I left them out by the paddock as you said the doe comes out there anyways."

"Okay – apples right by the paddock."

"Except Candy ate most of them." (Candy was one of the draught horses.)

Ivan said nothing, reflected on this, and then gave a sigh.

"But," Cindi said, "I saw some tracks –"

"Saw some tracks. Good, where did you see some tracks –"

"I'll show you," Cindi said, smiling in self-delight.

After supper they walked out into the field. Behind them, snorting now and then, was Troy, plodding the cold earth.

"Here," Cindi said, in triumph. "The tracks!"

Then, seeing the look on Ivan's face, she put her head down, as if she had been accused of something.

Ivan often noticed this about her and decided it must have come from her epilepsy.

"Those are good tracks," Ivan said, sitting on his haunches. "And everything like that there, except they're rabbit tracks – but no matter – we know where the rabbits are. I was wondering if there were any left about here – so now I know – well, mister man, she'll be a different story this winter than last – because we have found our rabbits, Cindi."

"Found our rabbits," Cindi said, her nose running from the cold. "Yes, we have found our tracks," she said.

But now everything had changed. At work he had a

19

pink slip. He had moved out of the apartment. Some nights he would go for long walks, but what did that matter? And people whom he didn't know looked at him, as if they knew all about him, and smiled.

There were other things also – those people whom he did not like seemed ready to express a gaiety when he himself was miserable.

It was true that he had seen Ruby's cousin Eugene visiting Cindi three nights ago – this was just before his pink slip. At work there had been some ore clogging the shute to the crusher. Men jabbed at it, and poked at it with no result, so Ivan, sweat and water running down his face, and his left ear seeming to be permanently twisted under his hard hat, stood upon it, jumping up and down.

The foreman told him twice to climb out of the bin, and he twice told the foreman that he would.

"Ya, ya," he kept saying.

Then, just when he was about to climb out, he took a final kick at a small piece of ore under his boot – to the left of his boot – which, in fact, he did not see as he kicked – and the tons of ore let go immediately beneath him. Now, when the ore let go, it seemed not to be under him, but, in fact, over his head, and he reached up and managed to catch a chain at the side of the shute and hold himself. Then, pulling himself over the bin, he walked away as if it hadn't happened. He simply went to the cage and surfaced, got in a Jeep and drove to the dry, stripped off and showered for a half-hour. Then for the rest of the afternoon he worked on his car in the parking lot behind the warehouse.

The parking lot was dry and empty, while the greying headframe sat heavy in the air. He had jacked the car up and was under it, when suddenly he was being kicked on the boots.

"What's this, a fuckin floater?"

"No," Ivan said, "I had a scare."

"You had a scare – you talk to your shift boss – you don't come out and steal my fuckin Jeep."

Ivan looked up and saw the man's legs, and then rolled himself out from under the car.

"Ya – well I had a fuckin scare," Ivan said, knowing he was talking to the mine's manager, and knowing instinctively that this was the one tactic that would save him. He simply turned, threw the wrench on the ground, kicked the jack out from under the car as if he was terribly annoyed, and walked back into the dry.

He was given a pink slip, but he knew in actual fact he could have been suspended. But the one thing about this experience is that he could not tell Cindi about it, because even if he did, it would not be the same – that is, everything about it would be told differently than he would have told the exact same story when they were together. Everything was different.

He left the mines the day after and never went back.

2

The next night he met his father Antony at Dr. Hennessey's. His father had arthritis in his left arm and was there to get a shot of cortisone. During the winter, Antony would use a small butane lighter to warm his left hand if he was out with the horses. His father was Allain Garrett's son; Ivan, however, had kept his mother's maiden name, Basterache.

Ivan felt responsible, not only for his father, but for his two sisters – Valerie, who was eleven, and Margaret, sixteen.

"I might seem to be a carefree individual," Antony said to him one night. "And sometimes I might be something of a carefree individual – the way I can wiggle my ears – but I have nothin since your mother left me. You'd think a woman would come home after seven years."

Antony would get into conversations with people who stopped to buy Valerie's worms in the spring. Valerie would sit out near the highway, a decent little girl of eleven, in a big hat, behind a huge cardboard box with a sign which read WORMS 4 SALE : 2 4 1 ON WORMS!

Ivan had noticed that Antony had gotten into what Ivan called "The World War Two Factor," and he would occasionally blame his lot in life on the fact that there was a bias against him because he was French.

"The only thing I was ever any good for was to bleed to death in a war – that's all they wanted me for," Antony said to a man, who was busy holding a night crawler in either hand. "And I went – I went – look at this here." And he would show a scratch on his forearm quickly.

"Where did you fight?"

"Just about everywhere."

"Who did you fight?"

"Almost everyone – I was at Dieppe – twice. I fought the Dieppenamese over at that place."

"Well, we all had to offer something during those years."

"Offer – I guess offer – but my kids are no good, and my wife took off with Clay Everette Madgill because he has money – so things are bad all around. No, I didn't mind fighting – don't get me so wrong on that – I believe in it –"

"How old are you now?"

"Forty-seven."

The man said nothing.

Antony sniffed and picked up a handful of worms, looking them over, and then told Valerie to go get some fresh earth.

"I look forty-seven – more closer to fifty-seven," Antony said. "In fact, almost sixty."

"I was going to say if you were just forty-seven, you'd be kind of young for the war."

"Well, it was a long son of a whore of a war," Antony said, as if the person had offended him and he no longer wished to talk. Then he looked so quizzically and angrily that the man decided it was time to leave.

"And don't be back," Antony said. "We'll sell our worms to those who know how to treat them!"

Now Antony was sitting on a chair with his feet up on Dr. Hennessey's desk. Aunt Clare, the doctor's sister-in-law, had let Ivan through the side door, so Antony didn't know he was there.

Ivan stood at the door, watching his father as Hennessey gave him the shot. There was a moon over the dark, stubbled lane, and hard snow still piled in the yard.

Antony rolled up his sleeve because he knew he was going to have his blood pressure taken. His arm was quite white, surprisingly to Ivan, who had hardly seen him with his shirtsleeves rolled up. And his shirt was opened, and his undershirt was the old-fashioned type with straps.

Ivan knew intuitively that Antony had been discussing him and the marriage that had fallen through. Dr. Hennessey took no interest in such talk.

But Antony had always told Ivan that Cindi was as "stupid as a fucking boot on a two-year-old. . . ."

He looked at his father's huge back, and the way his head was bent, and the way the room's shadow played on the back of his reddish neck. His father had marvellously sad eyes, and Ivan could forgive him almost everything because of that.

Doctor Hennessey looked bored with the talk and stood in salt-and-pepper slippers and his old khaki pants that were held up by a gigantic belt, and wearing a big red bow tie that seemed to wrinkle his Adam's apple more than usual. He was standing off in the darkness of the study. The darkness rested on the table and on the brand-new table lamp, which glowed greenly in the late-evening room.

When Antony noticed Ivan, he winked.

Then he said to Dr. Hennessey: "Now you did this here, and helped me out – I'm going to come over tomorrow with a load of fill."

"Well, I don't believe I need fill, Tony," the doctor said.

"What – of course you need fill," Antony said. "You could use some on your front yard."

Antony turned, his heavy black wallet linked to a chain on his belt and protruding out of his back pocket. Then he stopped by the door and grabbed Ivan by the shoulder, saying for some reason with tears in his eyes:

"Now this young lad just beat the shit out of his wife – so I have to go straighten him out."

The old doctor, puffing on his pipe, turned away furiously. Ivan said nothing. There was nothing to say.

Once outside, Antony was angry about the fill.

"Well – why did you offer it to him then?" Ivan said.

"Well, you know how he relishes what I do for him – first I have to ask him, and then I have to do all the dirty work."

So with that, Ivan didn't say anything else.

Tonight Antony had a plan – in fact, he always had a plan – he couldn't go without a plan of some kind, and like people who are always watching out for themselves, this plan might change in midstream if any other direction suited him. As Ivan, who was always a loner, noted about his father, his father couldn't do without a plan, or a partner. His partner in the last few months was Gordon Russell, whom he happened to be selling porno movies for – which he didn't think Ivan knew about, except Ivan had found them under his father's bed, and in his suitcase. Ivan wouldn't care except he did not like Gordon, because Gordon was one of the men who had had his mittens on Cindi.

The day before, Antony had cut his horse's hoof and wanted Ivan to take a look at it. He had cut Rudolf's left hind hoof. Rudolf had been Ivan's horse, but Antony had beat him at a game of horseshoes when he was eleven and took it. Antony had bet him the sleigh for the horse.

It was the only horse Ivan ever owned. However, he gave riding lessons at Madgill's and had broken Tantramar for Ruby Madgill last year.

Rudolf was a Belgian. Antony had bobbed its tail so tight that when Ivan was young, he thought it would cut off blood to its head. So he used to sneak out at night to look at it. There Rudolf would be all alone, its one pile of manure looking lonely in the centre of the floor.

Antony worked it day and night. He hired it out for sleigh rides, with twenty screaming, mittened children aboard, and with a pair of deer antlers attached by a strap to its head, while Antony was dressed in a red suit with black buttons.

"Are you a Santa?"

"Fuckin right."

He took it into the woods – and whenever he got drunk, which was almost continually, he tried to sell it down river. He would kick it, and then order it to bite his ear off to make people respect him. Though a strong horse, it was small, and Antony had tried to pass it off as a quarter horse to a young girl from the air base who wanted to take riding lessons. Ivan had heard about this in time, just as Antony was about to sell it, and came down and had to put his father in a headlock right in front of the girl.

"Yer squeezing my fuckin ears off."

"Tell her what it is."

"No."

"Tell her."

"No."

In many ways Antony had lived by his wits his whole life through.

"Give us a ride home – I want to show you Rudolf," Antony said.

"Why?" Ivan said. He was looking up the road, almost as if he expected Cindi to pop out of the woods and come running to him with her black eye. They were standing at the bottom of the doctor's lane, in the middle of a long turn, tangent to some small bare trees.

In the car going down river, Antony tried on a bunch of watches that he was supposed to sell. As soon as they got into the car he hauled them out – he had a whole pocketful. He held them up to his ear. Then he held them up to Ivan's ear.

"Go way," Ivan said. "I'm trying to drive the cocksuckin car."

"Don't tell me I don't know my watches," Antony said.

"They're all about a hundred dollars a piece – I imagine," Ivan said.

Then Antony berated all of his family, starting with Ivan, for not listening to his experiences over the years – that he had at least two-dozen experiences that no one listened to. This was not a new charge that he levelled. He had always felt that his family did not care for him – except for Valerie, whom he doted upon.

Their situation was this. Ivan's mother, and now Antony's ex-wife, Gloria Basterache and he had boarded Ivan out as a boy. He had beaten the snot out of him, and now Ivan was a man. They did not know one another.

"So," Antony said, after some reflection, looking out towards the bay, "you and Cindi are on the outs, I hear."

"I don't want to talk about it –"

"Just being parental."

"I don't want to talk about it."

"Very best." There was a silence. "She's a dumb quiff anyhow."

The moon was high over the trees. Its light cast over the yard. From the shed, Ivan and Antony could see one upstairs light on in the middle of the house. Ivan looked at Rudolf's hoof. Then he found a nail and cleaned the horse's hooves.

"So you were out on the road with him," Ivan said, cleaning the left hind hoof carefully and looking at the cut.

"I had him out for a little bit," Antony said.

"You didn't cross over the old bridge by the bog?"

"How did you know that? You been spying on me?"

"He's picked up a three-inch square nail. So how would he do that – I figure you were out on the cock-suckin bridge."

"He won't haul right – he never learned anything," Antony said, going about the horse and kicking it now

28

and then. The horse started to move back, but Ivan said, "Whoa boy."

Then Antony sat on a bale of hay. Then he stood up, and smoothed the hay out carefully and sat down again.

"That bridge is going down someday – you shouldn't be putting a horse on it," Ivan said.

The door had been left open and moonlight came in on the old stall. Some sawdust, as white as fine powder about the edges but hard and yellow at the top, was piled behind the half-opened door that had a broken hinge. Some fox mash sat in the wheelbarrow, and now and then Antony's few ginger-coloured foxes yelped. Both Antony's thumbs were taped where the foxes had bitten him. They bit him almost every day of their existence. And by the time fall rolled about, his fingers were usually too sore to skin them, so he had to get Ivan to do it.

Ivan wore his jean jacket, the sleeves rolled up near his elbows. Though small, his arms were very strong, and he had the tattoo of his nickname "Jockey" on his forearm. He had a few homemade tattoos on his knuckles that he had scratched out in defiance to Father LeBlanc – a short, untempered, colicky priest who had the charge of him for a year and a half in Tracadie. His friends at the boarding school in Tracadie had called him "Jockey." However, no one else did.

He bathed and wrapped the horse's hoof.

"You should have the vet over," Ivan said.

"No, God, you got her good," Antony said.

Antony then said, with unbridled pride and affection, "Valerie's got a training bra now. So she'll probably show it to you – she's been walking about the house with her chest pounced out for two weeks – she won't even wash it."

Then he smiled, and was silent. A strong short gust of wind came up over the yard.

"So – I was thinking we should go pick up Ernie and drink some booze," Antony said. "No sense in it going to waste – having it dry up or something." Antony's face broke into a big grin, and he did what he always did since Ivan was a child – he wiggled one ear up and the other ear down at the same time, faster and faster. "Yer some cute, Ivan," he said, "with that little prick-topped haircut."

When they went out, Antony shut off the light in the shed. Then, as if he had to show fastidiousness in front of his son, he went in and straightened an old studded collar and bridle. Ivan remembered the first time Antony had gone into Clay Everette Madgill's barn, he was standing beside him. His father's face beamed with joy at such a barn and the beautiful quarter horses, and he kept saying: "Someday now I'll have a barn like this."

Now Antony fidgeted carefully with his faded, studded bridle.

And Ivan felt sad as Antony walked towards the house.

Now there were three in the car. Ernie was with them. They had gone to his house to get him.

"I'd like to know why yer grouchy mother won't let you out of the house more," Antony said.

"I don't know either," Ernie shouted over the sound of the worn-out muffler. Ernie's whole appearance was grey. His hair was grey and combed straight back, his cheeks were sunken. He wore black pointed cowboy boots that came over the top of his grey pants. His knees were bony, and cigarette ashes fell on the zipper of his polished black leather jacket that allowed him, at age forty-four, to retain the demeanour of a teenage boy. "I don't know why she don't let me out to town," he said.

"Well, come to think of it, perhaps it's because yer a fuckin nuisance," Antony said.

Ivan said nothing. He shook his head. It was going to be a long night.

They parked behind the church to drink. An hour passed. Then two hours.

The priest looked in the car window at them. They were silent.

"Boys, I'll tell you this – you shouldn't be here pissing in my graveyard."

"I wasn't pissing, Father," Antony said. "Ernie was."

Ivan looked over at the church, which retained in the dark its bulked whiteness.

"I'll fight," Ernie said to the priest. He was sitting in his black leather jacket in the back seat. It looked to the priest as if the jacket was filled with impounded air, and only the head of a grey-haired whizzled teen-aged boy poked out of it. "I'm Cindi's uncle – I'll fight –"

Ernie was not Cindi's uncle but he had known her as a child, and it seemed appropriate now, because they had been talking about her, that he be her uncle.

"You got no right to bother those who've lived on the Gum Road!" Ernie roared at the priest. Then he said, "Let me out of this car!"

"We're going," Ivan said.

They moved back up the church lane towards the highway. Ernie was singing Elvis's "In the Ghetto," and

31

when he came to the second verse, he broke down and started to cry.

Antony told them he knew where there was a party.

They went to Clay Everette Madgill's house. Through the window they could see Ivan's mother, Gloria Basterache. She had married Clay Everette six years ago.

"Toldja there was a party goin on," Antony said.

"I don't see Cindi there," Ivan whispered.

Gloria walked about smiling – she seemed to be smiling at someone in the corner. She was standing in the glassed-in upper deck that rose on white pillars above the patio, which was still covered in a crust of hard snow, and housed a couple of wooden lawn chairs. Even to Ivan, her son, she was something of a goddess. He used to wait for her outside the church at Christmas time. He'd have his sisters with him, and have their hair brushed. Then their mother would come down from Clay Everette's in her mink stole, with snow coming out of the glistening sky and falling, falling gently on the dark, cold trees on Bartibog Island and on the mink's shiny glass eyes.

After a while, Ernie started to roar and yell. Then he threw a lawn chair and fell facedown in the mud.

They carried him back to the car. The moon was full and high above them. After some time driving about, Ernie got out and lost his teeth in a snowbank.

Then they were all out digging in the snow. Some trees snapped, for the wind was beginning to stiffen.

"Momma'll be some grouchy if I lose my teeth."

"Tell that sawed-off midget mother of yours to go fuck herself," Antony said.

Then they all got back into the car and drove on.

"I'll never take that Ernie out again," Antony said after he and Ivan were alone. "He ruins just about everything –"

"Did you know?" he said as an afterthought.

"What?"

"It's what Ruby told me – Cindi's got one in the oven. And what the hell is she going to do with it!"

3

It was two nights later. Nevin, Vera's husband, sat on a stool in the kitchen of Allain Garrett's house looking through the door at the rest of them, who were in the living room watching hockey. He had come to ask Antony for their money back. Antony had figured that by this time it would have been polite for him to have forgotten about it altogether. He had borrowed it almost six months ago.

The living room was lighted up by the TV set. A planter sat in the dark atop a rickety metal bookshelf. A large, coloured picture of the Pope and a crucifix hung above the couch, with yellow palm leaves stuck in the picture frame. The whole room smelled of toast. The telephone table, directly in front of Nevin, was littered with crime magazines, *Two Girls and the Robbery Suspect* and *The Case of the Clever Cleaver* – which little Valerie continually snuck up to her room – and a big cardboard box filled with pieces of an old orange rug sat against the coffee table.

Antony lived at home with his parents, where the old woman could cook for him and his children. His father, Allain, and his mother had had eleven children. Except for Claude, whose whereabouts no one knew, and Antony, who lived right at home, they had all done well.

The walls were dark, and a trophy of some sort, for 1930, sat in the hallway on the floor near the closet. The living room was dark but the kitchen was bright, the tiled kitchen floor scrubbed clean.

Valerie sat in the corner, eating toast with her nightie on. Her sixteen-year-old sister Margaret was sitting on the stairs with her physics book in her lap.

Antony's parents realized that there was a falling out between Nevin and their son, and they were very worried because of it. And children react instinctively to how adults feel. So Valerie, who was wearing a training bra under her nightie, looked up at Nevin morosely as she bit into her toast. Margaret, however, spoke to him when he sat down as if there was nothing wrong at all.

Nevin had to turn about to speak to her, and every time he did he could see her kneecaps through the banister. Then he took out a package of cigarettes and asked everyone in the room individually if they would like one, even Valerie, who just shook her head. Then Valerie said something to Margaret in French and burst out laughing. She laughed with that giddiness eleven-year-olds have. Then she put both hands over her mouth, and in this way seemed to embellish every moment of her hilarity, which all seemed to be directed at Nevin.

Then Allain said three words in French to his granddaughter and she got up and went upstairs. Then he turned about and smiled at Nevin apologetically.

There was a stew cooking on the stove. Another short phrase came from Allain in French, and once more Valerie appeared. She walked by Nevin as if it were his fault she had been subdued, and took a plate from the kitchen cupboard.

"Is Antony here?" Nevin said.

There was an unpleasant silence, so much so that Nevin was made to feel he shouldn't have asked the question. Valerie, very carefully, so as not to spill any, walked with the plate of stew into the porch. She half closed the old porch door and Nevin could hear voices. He could hear her speak to someone, and he could hear Antony answer in a whisper: "*Non, non –* Val –" And then muffled laughter. Then he distinctly heard someone take a mouthful of stew and swallow.

Then there was a car on the highway, a truck, a tractor trailer. All of these seemed to roar past the house at once, as if some sort of indictment had been passed on Nevin with the noise they made.

Nevin stood and walked over to the door, and, standing there, said in a shaking voice:

"Antony, I know you're there – I know!"

Nevin turned and smiled at the old folks. Allain's dark fingers holding the cigarette Nevin had just given him, and the tufts of hair, sticking up on the little old man's head, seemed also to be an indictment against Nevin.

"Antony, I know you're there!" Nevin said again.

There was a long moment of silence, felt by everyone, and finally the sound of someone slurping tea. This bothered Nevin so much he buttoned his coat the wrong way and left the house.

As soon as he left, Antony came out of the room to get himself another plate of stew.

He didn't speak to any of them, but assumed a look of having accomplished a great deal. Margaret, feeling that he would order her to do something, stood and tiptoed upstairs. The only problem was that at the far end of the hall she turned left, by force of habit, and walked into the wall. There used to be a door to the bathroom there, but Antony had walled it up two days before and made the door next to his room.

Margaret swore and yelled out in French that she had just broken her nose, and Valerie burst out laughing – uncontrollably, as she had earlier in the evening.

Antony, shaking his head as if everyone should know that he had walled up the door, walked back into the porch.

There was a short silence.

Then Antony said something to Valerie, and it started her giggling all over again, so much so that they finally had to say "boo" to her and give her sugar.

A week later Antony walked down the path by the old sleigh for the Belgian horse with the tail he tied up with twine. He kicked at a block of wood, and threw it up on the back of the woodpile as if angry about something. Then he hauled his pants up and continued on his way. Ivan had gone up to town that morning, received his severance pay, and had finally gotten the money for Nevin.

Antony found Vera and Nevin sitting in the living room. Vera was three months pregnant. For a long time she had been unable to get pregnant – so that all the men on the road used to tell Nevin that they would come down immediately and help him out. But after all the doctors made all the tests, and they became reconciled to the fact that they would never have a child, Vera became pregnant.

Antony came in and looked at them a moment. "I'm having one hell of a hell of a time," he said quickly.

"What's wrong?" Nevin asked.

"Oh, I been talking to that Ivan," Antony said as he sat on the corner of the couch, "and I think I'll have to move outta the house and move in with him – to straighten him around – for if I don't straighten that man out, he'll be dead."

"Dead," Nevin said.

"All he wants to do now is party – out partying all the time – while he has a retarded girl sitting in her apartment twiddlin her thumbs."

Then Antony, who if anyone in the world had asked him when he was walking down the path what he was going to say would not have been able to tell them, sighed and moved his sapphire ring about on his left hand.

"Why – what's going on," Vera said.

"He slaps the snot out of her and everything else like that there," Antony said. "And she as pregnant as a butterball. I told him – I told him, yer diggin yer own grave, making yer own bed, if you're going to hear the music you have to pay for the tune, there's more than one way to skin a cat, and lie down with dogs you'll wake up with fleas – but he listens to nothing."

Vera and Nevin still believed that Antony had been in the war – and a war hero – as he told them when they first moved here. He fought "the Dieppenamese," as he had told them, and had been wounded. "At Normandy – a hunk of times." He walked into Brussels in 1944 where he was "shot and left for dead."

38

When they had first moved here, he had been the first to visit them. Because of his advice, they wouldn't buy mackerel from one fellow, or have their garbage picked up by another. "Don't buy mackerel from that son of a bitch," he would say. "He's out every day robbing other people's nets. Garbage – I guess he picks up garbage, and he has a dump filled with chemicals and all of that that is killin us all off – it's in our well and I hadda rush Valerie to the hospital to have her stomach pumped up. Garbage," he said suspiciously, "I guess it's garbage – well, you know yerself I ain't saying nothin new under the sun."

So they paid Antony to pick up their garbage and bring them mackerel.

"Is there anything we can do to help?" Vera said.

"Ha – is there anything we can do," Antony said, as if suddenly angry with them both. "What do you guys think *I* been trying to do? The priest is no good whatsoever – he won't listen to reason – balded me out – Ernie and I went down to see him about it – the other night, as a matter of fact."

"What did he say?"

"Well," Antony said, "he just told us to get off his property –"

"I don't care for priests," Vera said. "How can they counsel anybody?" Vera liked to think she had a more humanistic vision than the one offered by the Catholic church.

And, sensing this about her, Antony said, sighing, "You think I do? Most are fruits."

"I didn't know you were having a bad time," Nevin said apologetically, "or I wouldn't have bothered you about the money."

"Bad time," Antony said. "Don't worry, boys and girls – it's nothing more than I went through all my life with no one to help me out, so I can manage once again, don't worry about me." And he laughed good-naturedly here because he suddenly believed everything he had just said.

"I brought you yer money back," he added, looking into his huge black wallet.

Nevin looked at him, then over at Vera.

"Well look, why don't you give us what you can and keep what you need," Vera said.

"Well – I can give you all except fifty to seventy-five dollars," Antony said, counting it out. "How's that?"

"That's all right," Nevin said.

Vera and Nevin both nodded to him, and then at each other.

"You were over the other night but I couldn't see you," Antony said. "I couldn't bring myself to come outta the room, and Daddy give me an awful time when you left."

Nevin didn't know what to say, so he only nodded again.

Again, Antony believed that everything he had said was true, when, ten minutes ago, he hadn't known what it was he was going to say. But it seemed that everything he said was said for a reason, all of which would become clear.

He walked back home, feeling somehow discontented with himself. He had planned to just give the money back and go away, but, as always, his nature to talk and to show himself in the best possible light no matter which direction it took, had overcome him, as it always did with people he secretly felt inferior to. And as always he felt discontented with himself afterwards.

"Well – I don't care what they think," he said to himself, as a man who always cares what people think will say. "I had to do everything since Gloria left – I always did."

He lowered his body to go under some brush and walked into his father's yard.

Valerie, who'd just gotten off the school bus, came into the house behind him. She took her tam off and folded it and put it on the table, and took her book bag and hung it up behind the door.

Antony's mother was peeling potatoes. The day was warm and Antony was walking about with his coat open, which was a sign of a warm day for everyone. Music came from the radio and old Allain was on the couch in the living room with his hand over his face. His head looked frail and tufts of grey hair stuck here and there, a final call for justice it seemed for a man who had worked by brute strength for seventy-five years.

Antony stopped and turned about in a complete circle, as if expecting somebody. Then he looked out the window at the highway.

"Where is Ivan?" he said.

His mother shrugged.

"Well, there's another big scrape he's into," he said. His little girl, who had poured herself a glass of milk and had a milk moustache, was busy sorting out which drawings she was going to pin on the fridge, and which of her last week's drawings she was going to take off the fridge and throw away, with the equanimity of a person who controls her own destiny.

"Beats up Cindi, who's knocked up as high as the proverbial kite, and then leaves her for me to take care of," Antony said.

As soon as he sat down, Valerie put her milk down and went over to the counter. She climbed up on it and got a cup. Then she walked on her knees along the counter to the oven mitts, which she put on, and picked up the huge glass teapot. Then after she had poured the tea, she jumped down and walked very carefully towards him.

He took the tea and blew at it, deep in thought. Then, without looking at her, he took out an Extra Big chocolate bar and handed it to his daughter. He stuck his tongue in his cheek to push it out and leaned into her for a kiss, all the while not looking her way.

"I gotta go up and see Gloria," he said.

And, after adjusting his ever-present welding cap, and with his hands in his pockets, he motioned with his head for Valerie to grab her coat and follow him.

They backed out of the yard in the truck and proceeded up the road, past the bootleggers', past the church lane, by the woodchop and the black spruce trees.

Every month Gloria gave him two hundred dollars, and every month he scrupulously took not a penny for himself but put it aside carefully for his daughters' needs.

There were teeth to be fixed and clothes to be bought, and allowance, and he scraped and saved and penny-pinched to get all of this done.

Now, after telling his ex-wife that he was trying to straighten their son Ivan out, and looking at her for a sign that she might be pleased with him because of this, she lay on the chesterfield with her eyes half-closed, he was sad once more.

"Do what you want, Tony – I've sacrificed enough," she said.

42

Her face looked pale, which always showed she was in a bad temper.

"I got Valerie out in the truck," he said.

"Ya – well tell her I'll see her," she said.

"When?"

"When – when – when I do. Every time you come here there's a problem."

Gloria had decided three years earlier that she wanted to bring Valerie to live with her. Valerie came to Clay Everette's carrying her own suitcase and a big doll. They enrolled her in gymnastics and swimming, and Gloria always did her hair.

One time she crawled in under the hay in the back of her father's truck and was found sleeping in her small bed the next morning, and another time she ran away and stayed with Ivan. Then she fell at gymnastics and loosened three teeth. Gloria bought her a puppy and her own horse, Smurfie, and then, finally, Gloria took her back to Antony. The little girl walked into the house, made herself a molasses sandwich, and sat at the table. This is what she had been about to do when Gloria had come to get her four months before.

Now Gloria lay with her housecoat on, which seemed to be designed in the fashion of some Eastern tapestry, and she settled one bare leg over the top of the couch's arm, with her hand behind her head.

Antony did not know what to say, and as always he seemed to say the wrong thing.

"It's just that the doctor is beggin me for some fill, and I was wonderin if I could get some topsoil from Clay," he said.

Gloria rolled on her side and punched the pillow.

"Beggin me for some fill," Antony said to himself.

Gloria looked up at him and said: "Clay won't refuse you anything – take it."

And Antony knew this was true.

Then, suddenly, feeling he had to say something, he said: "That Ivan is gonna be the death of you, isn't he? Wife-beatin cocksucker."

"He's already been the death of me," Gloria said, yawning.

"That's what I told him – I said, 'Don't think of me if you don't want, but yer gonna kill yer mother.'"

There was a silence. Then his voice shook. "I said, 'I put yer mother through hell – so for Godsakes, don't you too.'

"You should go to the doctor," he said after a moment. "If I see Clay Everette, I'm going to give him a piece of my mind about getting you to Armand for a good check-up."

Armand Savard was the doctor a lot of younger people went to, and Gloria as well. He drove a Porsche and was at the beach most of the summer, had a chronic tan, and was known, all of a sudden, as the best doctor on the river.

Then Antony said: "I bet if you sent Ruby over to look in on Cindi – and see that that Ivan stays the hell away from her –"

Ruby was Clay Everette's daughter from his first marriage, and Antony suddenly looked upon her as fondly as any of his own.

"Yes – yes, I'll send her along," Gloria said.

When Antony walked back to his truck, the day was getting colder. Shadows came down on the patches of mud. There were grey shadows on the inside of his truck and on Valerie's tam.

"You know you should have come in to see Mommie," Antony said.

The girl, with her skinny legs covered in red leotards, and her tam pressed down onto her small ears, looked at him and shrugged.

For some reason Antony blushed, and as he drove home tears came to his eyes.

4

Cindi had always been considered slow, although she was always perceptive enough to the care of herself. She was an epileptic – a petit mal, though a bad petit mal. She had spent two years in grade ten and two years in grade eleven, and finally graduated because of the policy of grace. She went at night to a tutor and worried over every Algebra equation, and every page of history.

She had stayed at the apartment after Ivan had left. It was an apartment building below Big Cove turn. Its windows looked glib in the winter and scorching hot in the summertime. It had the appearance of a prefab school for elementary grades, without the advantage of grass or shrubs.

There was one shrub out back that she had planted, which had been covered with burlap all winter. Below her the road went straight down river, narrow and calved with frost heaves. She could see the nearest light of Loggie's wharf when she stood upon her tiptoes.

She still had a swollen eye and some bruises. She had gotten them when she had fallen down the night of the fight. Ivan had put an ice pack on her eye, had taken off her clothing as he did after all her seizures. When she woke up she ran. She ran about the building four or five times and then went to Ruby's to spend the night.

She was pregnant. She did not want to bring another child home to her mother. And now, because of what had happened, she was scared she would have to. She was resolved never to rely upon her mother or anyone else ever again. Like some people who are considered slow, she could be quite stubborn. Her mother was frightened for her. Everything her mother feared had come true – because her mother had always believed the worst about her.

"This is a terrible time in her life, and she has nowhere to turn. But there will be no child if she doesn't want it – you just mark my words," she'd overheard Ruby say to Dr. Savard. And this, somehow, gave her a shivery feeling and made her feel important. "There will be no child if I don't want it," she whispered.

The outrage of others made her feel important. It was impossible not to feel this way, with so many people concerned about her and visiting her, and Ruby saying: "Leave her alone – let her rest for a while."

Margaret Garrett had tried to visit, and Gloria had come over. Adele had phoned and said she would be down. A woman's group had phoned to see if she needed money. There was a talk show on local television about a transition house, and her case, but not her name, was brought up by a woman with close-cropped hair whom she didn't even know. (This woman happened to be Vera.)

But the people who rushed in and out of her life at this time, and made her, suddenly, as Antony would

47

say, "The most important show on the road," had no idea that they partook in humiliating her. In fact, if they had been told this, they would deny it with that tumultuous anger that liberal thinkers often mistake for concern over human rights.

And yet she felt also that she had finally become important to people she had always looked up to, who had never liked her.

Even Antony went to see her. He came in one Saturday morning.

"Well – how are you?" he said.

"I'm all right," Cindi said.

"You don't look beaten up too bad," he said. (As if he wanted her to be more beaten up for effect.)

"No," she looked at him and then looked at her fingers and wobbled them together. The day was cooling off, and a mute sky lay flat against the water. She had tried to comb out her perm that Ruby had gotten for her, and now her hair was curly in one place and straight in another. Her eyelashes kept blinking.

"An awful thing," he said. He sat down on the edge of the couch and took a deep breath.

Every now and then she would look up at him and blink, and then look down again.

"Cup of tea?" he said after a long moment.

Cindi, who had always tried to show everyone that she was useful and could do things like her friends, jumped up and literally ran out to the kitchen to make him tea.

He drank some tea and looked at her. He looked very closely at her, but he couldn't see any marks. She sat with her knees pinched together.

"So," he said, "you got a hot cross bun in the oven."

Cindi smiled, and again folded her hands on her lap. Then she tried to tell a story about what she and Ivan had planned to do, and where they would live. "But then," she said, in a whisper, "we got in a fight."

Antony then told her he remembered that fifteen years ago the Defoe boy was born with his right ear inside his brain, and his left ear deaf.

Cindi looked at him, blinking, and tried to think.

"Was it sticking out?"

"Was what sticking out?"

"Its ear?"

Antony shook his head. "Turned side on in its skull, I heard."

He drank his tea as his eyes wandered over the apartment. In the twilight, the apartment empty, the evening light cast on the bar stool in the corner with the poignancy of spring. Some birds complemented it by a twitter or two, and there was a smell of slush in the lane.

Cindi, like many people when the first warm weather comes, was wearing a sleeveless blouse and now shivered.

"What does Ivan think of it?" Antony said.

"I don't even think he knows," Cindi said. "I wasn't sure until a week ago."

Then with a voice that startled even himself, Antony said, "Ho, ho – he knows – don't you kid yourself on that. I was up at the doctor's the other night, and he was there."

"What did he say?" Cindi said nervously, as a person who only wants people to say kind things about them.

"Dr. Hennessey asked me to speak to Ivan about you, but of course Ivan was all worked up about gettin drunk with me."

"Drunk?"

"Well – I tried to speak to him aboutcha, and being pregnant, and he said, 'Don't you worry about her – I need to get some booze and that's what we should be talking about!'"

Cindi didn't speak, and the napkins she had brought in with the tea and cookies added character to her little body.

"Don't you worry about Ivan though – I'll take care of him," he said suddenly. "I can handle that boy."

"I don't want anything bad to happen to him," she said. And in spite of herself, she smiled self-importantly.

"I told them when you announced the wedding," he said, under his breath. "Clay called me over and said he was going to get you some furniture. I said, 'Furniture them all you want, but that little girl is going to marry the wrong man.'"

Cindi stared straight ahead blinking. Then she picked up a cookie and took a nibble.

She felt sad for everyone suddenly.

Antony then said that he took responsibility for his son, and when he did he spoke in a resigned way.

And Cindi was uncomfortable on his behalf.

✛   ✛   ✛

On April 30, Adele drove down river to see what was going on.

She arrived at the apartment just after Ruby came in. Ruby was telling Cindi that her cousin Eugene was home for the summer and she wanted her to see him more often. She had always said that Dorval Gene and Cindi loved each other. "Everyone knows that," she would say. She called him "Dorval Gene" because he was from Montreal.

As far as Ruby was concerned, Cindi should go out. She told her about the horse-hauling at the community centre, next week, and she should go to the dance and have some fun.

Ruby said what people always said on these occasions as if there never was a personal motive for saying it. When Cindi didn't know if she would go or not, Ruby asked for Adele's advice.

"Well Delly – what do you think?" she said, as she started to comb Cindi's hair out with a brush, while Cindi kept wincing.

"I think Cindi can make up her own mind if she wants to go out or not," Adele said, thinking that this was a very wise answer, and going over to hold Cindi's head.

"Well, of course," Ruby said, "we all know that," and looked at Adele as if she wasn't as bright as she had once thought.

Cindi sat in the chair looking from one to the other.

Ruby was very pretty. She also had a coarseness, which added to her beauty. She had been captain of the women's hockey team at the community centre, before she went to university, and she knew how to take care of herself on the ice, to butt end, to spear, and to take a woman out in the corners. She used to sit in a faded T-shirt and jockstrap in the dressing room after a game, with a small diamond earring stud in her nose, putting her equipment away, her legs and throat covered in sweat, nonplussed at the coming and going of young men who could see over the partition. The

51

diamond stud in her nose added to the sharpness of her eyes.

"We have to get her out of this hole now and again," Ruby said to Adele when they left the apartment. "You should know that."

"Yes," Adele said, "of course that's right."

And, of course, it was. As Vera had said on the local television, and this was true as well, people like Cindi had the court of world opinion on their side. And so they should.

As they left the building, birds flew to the trees outside and gave sound to the late-April air.

✣   ✣   ✣

Ruby had a stud horse called Tantramar, and a colt called Missle, after the boy she once almost married. Ruby fell in love and the boy had died. It was a long time ago. But when she smelled the leaves under the rock wall near her back lane, she thought of him.

He didn't have very much – not like Ruby herself – nor had he ever had a girlfriend, something which Ruby had thought hilarious. Every summer it seemed to be someone new for her. Her boyfriends never lasted.

But she loved Missle. He didn't drink – which was a drawback – but he didn't take her credit cards. And he did love her.

One night, by the rock wall near the lane in back of her father's house, she explained all about her boy-friends.

"I've had a lot of boyfriends," she said.

He won't never be back, she thought.

But he did come back.

He did come back. He looked like a private in the army, with his hair short, his mouth small, his eyes dark and wide.

She often told him she was spoiled.

"You're not spoiled at all," Missle said, and he could hardly get the words out.

"Well, all I ever want to do is party and have a good time," she said. "What do you want to do?"

"I want to become a speech therapist," he said.

He was so slight she felt that she had to protect him. She knew no one would dare bother him if he was with her.

She wrote about him to her cousin, Dorval Gene, and told her friends about him. Cindi would be her bridesmaid, and they would live in Halifax, and she would work and he would go to school.

He tried to do things, which would have exasperated her in any other man. But with him, she was patient, even parental. He had to get her to teach him how to ride a horse because she rode. He got up at five in the morning. He would go around the arena, she would watch him hopefully. Ivan Basterache would shout instructions and encouragement, and then he would just slide off, as if his hip bones weren't big enough to support him.

He wanted to be a speech therapist because he had never learned to talk until he was nine years old. He had lived in his own world.

Ruby, who was always making fun of people, now learned not to do this in front of him.

He was so naive that she tried to protect him from everyone, especially from former boyfriends, who would ask sexual questions about her.

One day, she put on a top hat and her old tap shoes, and tap-danced for him in the living room.

"Look," she kept saying, her face perspiring and her eyes closed shyly. "See – what I – can do," she kept saying.

And she was using an old broom handle as a cane.

"I love you as the grass is green," he said.

And tears came to his eyes, and she had to stop and put her arms around him, and comfort him, like a child.

He died two nights later, in his sleep.

She became more beautiful than ever after that, and lost herself in regret, tantrums, envy, and physical abuse from married men. Now she had a crush on Dr. Savard.

They had met for the first time the month before. She was wearing an old grey coat and a pair of work boots because she was down river with her father. It was raining, and the rain fell over the white hard hat she had pulled down over her eyes. She had an acetylene torch in her hand.

There was snow on the ground, and the wind smelled of ice in the frozen rain. She moved towards her father's truck in the dark. If she had gotten a drive home with Lloyd, her father's foreman, as she had on the previous two nights, she would have missed him.

But as she waited for her father, Armand Savard came out of the rain towards her. She gave a start because he looked something like Missle, except his skin was darker, like an Acadian's. In fact, Missle had a blemish on the side of his chin – and just on that side, Savard had one also, a little darker perhaps. These marks were signs of premature birth. Missle had been two months premature and so, too, had Savard.

Just the day after she met Adelē, she was sent with a load of old tires to a warehouse down river. The streets were broken up, the bay was dark. There was a lonely sea gull sitting on the pier. Suddenly the sun came out cold and caught a window above her and sunlight hit her eyes. She turned about and saw an apartment building across the road. There was an ugly window that looked out onto a dirt parking lot.

It did not enter her mind at the moment, but over the course of time and events, the apartment building, Cindi, and Savard would all seem to fuse together.

5

Antony walked up the church lane with his daughter Valerie by the hand. He was puffing, and every now and again he would stop to cough.

It was at these times, when alone with her that Antony would tell Valerie about his youth. He would tell her how he worked in a hotel in Toronto when he was sixteen, and how he swam the river with his brother Claude, or how a friend got killed in the hold of a ship in Millbank – the dry pulpwood on that far-off 1955 June day, which seemed only a second removed when he remembered it, falling an inch from his own skull. He would talk to her about the road and the river, and how everything was growing bigger.

He stopped to find a Chiclet for her, covered her little hand with his big one, and they continued on their way.

When they got home, his daughter took her brownie uniform off and put it in the closet. Later, Antony went up to her room and, getting on his knees with her, said two and a half prayers – that is, two Hail Mary's and a half of the Our Father.

Then, tucking the little girl in and collecting every doll in the room to put on her bed, plus the transistor radio so she could listen to her "Hour of Power" rock program, he went in to see his older daughter, Margaret.

"Yer not hanging about with all those boys," he said to her.

"*Garçons?*" she said, looking up.

"You know what boys – Bramble Much and that crew."

"No," she said. She stared at her father with a great deal of indifference, but he didn't notice this.

"Good – you help Val wash her hair tomorrow morning before you go to school."

He went into his room and sat on the edge of the bed, just as he had sat there since he was three years of age. In fact, except for the bed getting bigger, the room hadn't changed. There was an alarm clock on the floor, near the box of Kleenex he always kept beside his bed, because he coughed all night, and a floor-model radio near the window with the curtains pinched back.

It was a lovely night in spring. You could hear the cars from a long way away splashing through the last of the snow that had run onto the road. The twilight lasted a long time, and the sky was warm. At dark, birds twittered here and there, one sitting on the oil barrel, a group of small sparrows in the tree, and a swallow darkly darting into and out of the shed. The window light also cast on the stones below, as if inviting all into this warmth.

He decided to clean out his wallet, laying things that he wished to throw out on the lopsided bed, with the pink covering, beside him.

Then he found a pen and scribbled down some things he would need for the upcoming horse-hauling.

Then, when he heard Frank Russell in the yard, he left the house. Frank had brought the truck around to take away Rudolf for the horse-hauling – he was going to team him with his own Belgian, Catterwall, which he had done before.

Antony was paid sixty dollars to rent the horse out for the hauling. The trouble was they had a hard time getting the old horse on the truck. It stood firmly in the mud, sideways to the truck with its ears back, breathing in a sombre way, a solitary member of its race standing alone in the little yard, haltered and blinking, with the bandages hanging from its hind leg, and its stomach covered in sawdust where it had lain.

It would neither eat an apple Frank tried to give it, nor react to Antony's kicks. Finally Antony, vest and jacket opened, hat tilted and boots untied, and the laces dragging happenstance in the mud, went in to get the pitchfork.

"We'll get you on the truck, mister fuckin man," he said.

Frank had already planned to guard his team very carefully for the next day's event, but he and his wife also planned to tea another team; his wife, Jeannie, being the one to put him up to it.

At this point, Antony stood, pitchfork in hand, standing under the lone light of the shed, with the smell of mud and the twittering frogs in the ditch – that is, all the sounds and smells of nostalgia.

Just then, Ivan drove into the yard and, with his car still running, came over to them.

"We're trying to get Dolfy into the truck," Antony said, moving back slightly.

"Yer not going to team him."

"Yes –"

"Oh for fuckin sure now," Ivan said. Then he spoke in French to Antony, but Antony, as a formal reprimand, answered him in English.

"His leg's the very best," Antony said. The weight of his statement fell upon the old blinkered and haltered horse, with its belly covered in sawdust.

Antony then snapped the flat side of the pitchfork against the horse's rump, but Ivan said, "Hold it!" And to Rudolf, "Get up in the box." He took Rudolf by the halter and smacked his lips, and kicked gently at his front left leg. The old horse turned about and walked up the plank.

"Oh, we're some smart," Frank said.

"I don't need to pitchfork a fuckin horse at any rate," Ivan said from the far side of the animal.

"Ya, well maybe I should cure you of being the big-feelinged lad," Frank said under his breath.

"Don't let fear stop you," Ivan said.

Antony looked at them and the horse in the box, sighed, and took the sixty dollars, two tens and two twenties.

At the horse-hauling there was an altercation. Ivan had come out of the woods, after going along the trap lines and picking up his sets, which he had hanging in the trees. He came out and got to the dance at 11:30.

When he saw Cindi dancing with Dorval Gene, he threw a chair at them and left.

Some time later, Jeannie Russell woke up to find Ivan with Rudolf and, thinking he was teaing the horse, attacked him with a crop as Ivan was leading him out of the stall.

Jeannie was a small, spiteful, nasty little woman who treated the horses worse than any man she knew would because this would prove her superiority. Her scorn for men was great. She and Frank kept vigil all night over the horses, slept beside them – accused others of doing what they themselves would do, and Frank was, in more ways than one, under her control.

Later Frank, with his raw-boned look – a reddish, almost fierce complexion – and his wife, standing tooth and nail beside his waist, fought against the small, deceptively strong Ivan Basterache, with the old half-blind horse, Rudolf, breaking through the paddock and clomping at a sort of half-halt, heavy-footed, down river, moving sideways along the road, back to its floor-dug shed. Cindi tried to stop the fight, which she believed had started because of her, and in doing so she was hit in the stomach. Other people joined in and beat Ivan to the ground for attacking his pregnant wife. Cindi went to the floor on one knee, like a boxer who had just been hit in the liver.

Because of what was happening to his son, Antony found himself catapulted into the fierce circle of rumour that he tried to control to his own benefit.

"What happened down there?" he asked Gloria.

They were sitting in her glassed-in porch that looked out over the dry highway.

"I don't know," Gloria said. "When was the last time you saw me at the community centre? Ruby's gone out to see her colt – you have to ask her."

But he shook his head, expecting the worst – in some secret perverse way – because his own life had been miserable, hoping the worst would happen to others.

Dorval Gene had said that Ivan threw a chair that missed them by a fraction, and that Ivan had run from the hall as if all courage had failed him, only to be found hidden behind a horse an hour later. This was the rumour that started to circulate.

"Now what in hell is Ivan up to?" Gloria said.

Antony just shook his head.

"It's all different now than when we were young," he said.

Far away across the field the trees were green, and the pulpwood in the field below was drying in the sun.

"Well, we can't live our children's lives for them," Gloria said. "They'll have to work their squabbles out." Then she added, "Clay just decided he's going to build Ruby a house."

"Ruby a house – God bless her."

"He says she's too old to be here and she mayswell have a house of her own," Gloria said.

"Of course," Antony said, "I can see that – she needs a house. . . ."

After talking a while longer, Antony went out to see Ruby.

Ruby had the colt chained and was brushing it.

"Tony," she said, "how are you?"

"I don't know," he said. "It's this trouble –"

Ruby frowned over the top of the colt. The little thing got skittery when Antony came towards it, its small head lifting rigidly up against the halter clamps.

"Yes," Ruby said, "he went down there last week and got into a big blowout – that's the tricks Ivan gets up to."

"Goddamn him," Antony said, without needing one more word of explanation but as if everything had already been proven to be true.

He paused for a moment.

"And that little girl pregnant," he said. "He's a coward."

"I know, I know," Ruby said, blowing a bubble with her gum and brushing the horse back from the withers. "He never thinks. Once again he could have killed her."

"Almost did," Anthony said.

"Just a bee-hair wide," Ruby said, "with that old chair."

In Clay Everette's yard, Antony's self-esteem always fell. He wanted to leave but he went back inside. Gloria was still sitting on the couch. There was the smell of boiled turnips and the whir of a fan somewhere. There was the long-tailed fluffy cat sitting beside her, and she was stroking its fur absent-mindedly with her red-painted fingernails.

Clay had gone to pick up a truck that he'd bid on tender the month before, so she was alone. He sat down on the smallest of the three chairs facing her.

"Tony, how's Margaret?" she asked suddenly.

She was drinking and her eyes were glassy.

"Oh, I don't know," he said. There was a smell of burning leaves that emanated through the long windows that made the sun hotter on his back, and he could see Gloria sweating as she tipped up the glass, and he saw her neck. "She's man crazy," he said.

"Poor Margaret," she said, and as she said it she clinked some ice at the bottom of the glass and looked down into it a second. "I could have taken her – she begged to come with me. Valerie was too young – I mean, we know that now. Now Margaret and I could have done things together." And the way she said "now Margaret and I could have done things together" was surprisingly shallow.

She finished her drink and looked about the room. Then she grabbed the cat by the fur and dug her fingernails into it. "Oh, scruffy cat," she said.

"Oh, scruffy cat," Antony said, reaching over carefully to pat it. "Our kids don't know who they are today – with all this shit going on," Antony said.

"No, they don't know who they are," Gloria said, getting up and walking into the kitchen, walking away from him so that he couldn't help staring at her hips, and, holding the glass in her hand, she clinked the melting ice. "But we tried – and we tried until we got tired of trying – and then," she said, as she poured another vodka out of the large side of the jigger, "we tried some more. But with you and I not getting along – and the money not coming in. Well," she said, biting a piece of celery, and wagging it, "no matter how we tried, it was out of our hands."

Then she came towards him, still wagging the celery. "But I'm still sorry I wasn't with Margaret when she was growing up – there's so much a woman could tell her."

And there was something about the phrase that was again false and meaningless, that came off television

63

sets and nights in bars or cottages, and had nothing to do with the magnificence of her daughter. Nor did she care that her voice was false. Then she sat down heavily on the couch and took a drink.

"We should have boarded Ivan out longer," Antony said. "If we could have kept him in school at Tracadie, it mightn't have been so bad on you."

"Ivan, I never got over the pain he put me through."

"I told him – I told him," Antony said, shaking his head bitterly.

"And now he's exactly crazy," Gloria said.

"Well," Antony said passionately, after a minute, "I knew you suffered but I didn't know the half of it. I should have trusted ya before – I shoulda – I shoulda trusted you before!"

Gloria finished her drink as if she were angry with it. Then there was a silence. Her eyes burned brightly and there was water in them. Then she stared up at him indifferently, as if he wasn't there.

Antony got home to the same house, the same walls, the same yard, with the ever-present sameness to the problems he had, leaving behind his other life. He took off his sapphire ring and placed it on the windowsill above the sink, and stared out at a flat bunch of alders and the old, rusted oil barrel across in the field.

He was quiet until he saw his oldest daughter.

"What in hell are you doing with your new slacks on?" he said.

She had come in through the back way, up through the woods, and had some mud on the bottom of her new slacks, which he had just gotten for her. He noticed how she had been looking at them as she walked, and how they bagged about her knees. The May heat lay against the window and in the corner of the room.

He did not know how furious he would become. But once fury starts it is hard to calm.

"Get up those stairs," he yelled. "Get up those stairs!"

Suddenly he started towards her. She backed away and then turned, saying something under her breath in French.

"What did you say?" he yelled. "What?"

He went towards her, but she ducked under him and then fell. When she did, he stood over her. His hands grabbed at her as she tried to kick her way up the stairs, and then he ended by ripping the pocket of her slacks. Old Allain tried to hold him by the arms, but Antony was too strong, and his mother kept saying that someone was in the yard, as she always did when she was frightened.

Margaret sauced him but not until she was alone. After a while he went to the supper table and ate. Every now and then he would put his fork down and shake his head at Valerie, as they listened to her cry.

❖   ❖   ❖

Ivan spent his time working on the engine of his grandfather's thirty-six-foot lobster boat. He had a wound over his left eye from Jeannie Russell's crop.

Frank Russell and his wife happened to own the meadow on the upriver side of the wharf, owned the field on the left of the road and put their cattle out to feed. Ivan would see the cattle moving about.

Sometimes he would not hear them and then look up and five or six cows would be looking at him from thirty feet away, standing up to their knees in fly-filled mud, chewing their cuds.

Now and again Jeannie would come down to count the cattle and look over at him, her coarse red hair pulled back behind her neck, her hearing aid visible, and her rubber boots flagging away doggedly as she walked across the muck.

She would shout at the cattle in that wild screech she had as she rounded them up, gumbooting herself across the muck with the determination of a small devil, insolent to everyone, and Frank coming down behind her; his fierce red complexion made more fierce still by his starched and weathered green work shirt. He, too, would glance Ivan's way, and then look at his small wife and nod – which always seemed more spiteful from a distance.

"How's Cindi?" Jeannie would yell after this nod. And Frank would stand beside her, grinning. "If you leave me, baby, can I come too," Jeannie would yell.

Sometimes Frank would bring his twelve-foot motor boat up to the wharf while Jeannie stood on the shale bank, her rubber boots dug into her property line, watching with a sort of nasty grimace.

"Ask him how Cindi is," she would yell.

Then Frank would walk up the hill while Jeannie walked before him, switching the cattle.

"Oh ha, oh ha," Frank would laugh. "Out runnin the roads with that Ruby Madgill."

Ivan usually went inside whenever he saw them. He'd sit on the cot in the murky heat of the cuddy and smoke a cigarette until he heard them leaving or at

66

least walking out of sight, and then he would come out again and do his work. He parked his car as far away from their property as possible.

One day, while waiting for them to go, Antony came in, looking terrible and leaning forward with his hat in his hand. "You didn't punch Cindi in the stomach when you were at the dance last week, did you?"

"Who in Christ told you that?"

"I was just wondering –"

"Who told you that!"

"It's all over the river –"

"What do you mean it's all over the river?"

And then Antony, with his mouth dry, said in a scared fashion: "Well, it's just inescapable that it would be – you know – all over the river. If you go about poking a pregnant woman in the guts, it sorta goes all over the river."

"No, I don't know that it would be inescapable that it would be all over the river. It's a lie, and so why should it be all over the river or anywhere else."

Ivan looked at his father and folded his arms.

"That's what people think," Antony said.

"For fuckin sure they would," Ivan said.

"It's what Ruby told me –"

"Well, you can believe what you want, I don't care. And that goes for Cindi as well."

"It disturbs people is all I can say."

"Well, people are going to say more than that about me," Ivan said. "The cunts always have and always will."

"Frank doesn't like you," Antony said, as if to affirm Ivan's statement.

"Not too many people do," Ivan said matter-of-factly.

"I told them," Antony said suddenly, as if he realized he must take Ivan's part. "I told Clay and Gloria and the whole crew of them. I said, I said, 'The whole buncha ya is just turned right against Ivan, and I'm not gonna stand here and listen to that there.'"

Ivan turned about and got some Ben Gay down from the drawer to put on his hands. He had hurt his back when he fell against the floor, and was rubbing some on it.

The bay was rolling gently and a wave of heat lay over the buoys. Far up the beach, where the clay walls of the bank met the black shale, Jeannie had gone to get the gelding.

"Haven't you seen Cindi?" Antony asked.

"I don't see Cindi and she don't see me," Ivan said. And then under his breath, "Every whore I get mixed up with has rocks for fuckin brains – you mayswell take them all and shove a peavey up their quiffs."

"Well, that's where your mistake is," Antony said. "You should see her – if you don't, things will only get worse."

Ivan turned and went out through the cuddy door into the sunlight. He went to the end of the boat and threw a bucket of potato peels into the water, and stood watching the black tide rise against the tar planking.

6

Ralphie had done all things in order to make others happy. He had moved into his mother's house on her request. He had opened a business downtown, he had joined the Kinsmen; he was not happy. And as he turned twenty-six, it seemed to him that he could be thirty-six or fifty-six and it wouldn't matter at all.

He knew his wife Adele wasn't happy either. She wasn't happy in the large house with nothing to do.

He knew Ivan would do anything for him or Adele – he knew, in fact, that Ivan looked upon him as a brother. There was an incident in their lives which Ralphie never forgot.

When he and Ivan worked back at the mines Ralphie was bullied by one man. Every day the man hid Ralphie's lunch, or filled it with ore, and made light of whatever Ralphie said or did.

One day Ralphie came to work in a new work shirt, and the man looked at the top button and said: "Do you want this?"

"Yes," Ralphie said, smiling.

So the man pulled it off and handed it to him.

"Do you want this?" the man said, touching the next button.

"No," Ralphie said. So the man pulled the button off and threw it away.

He continued until all the buttons were pulled from the shirt. Ralphie had to pretend that this was a joke that he himself appreciated, and that all the other men and he laughed at this in the same fashion.

It was not until a month later that Ivan learned about this. Ralphie did not tell him, or complain to him, but Ivan finally saw what was going on. He never once said that Ralphie should be ashamed for not standing up for himself, and he never mentioned it to him in any way. But Ralphie was frightened of getting hurt in some way, and every time the man teased him, he instinctively weighed the alternative.

One afternoon, when Ralphie was in the dry, the man walked towards him, his pale blue eyes unfocused – and as soon as he realized Ralphie was there he turned immediately and went in the opposite direction.

"He'll not bother you again," Ivan said on the way home that night. "Gutless fucker."

Ivan said nothing else and Ralphie never had to thank him.

Ralphie had almost forgotten this incident. Until now. Now he tried not to think of it. But last week when Ivan pulled up in his car in front of the shop, Ralphie pretended to be out.

When Ivan couldn't find Ralphie, he went to see Adele to ask her if she had talked to Cindi. It was the first

70

time they had met in a year, and Adele was sitting in the den when he drove up in his car.

"Who is that?" Thelma asked. The car's fender was smashed, and the window had a pebble crack in it. The tires were almost bald. It was as if he had come out of another world entirely and entered theirs through some other, heated atmosphere.

"Oh, that's a friend of ours – you know him – Ivan," Adele said.

"Ivan who?" Thelma said, in the same immediate and accusing voice she always had when dealing with her daughter-in-law.

"Ivan Basterache," Adele said.

"I don't know him," Thelma said. "I have only heard bad things about him."

"Of course you do," Adele said. "You met him at Ralphie's apartment a long time ago, and he came to our wedding."

Ivan had gotten off work late on the day prior to Ralphie and Adele's wedding. He was working in Port Hawkesbury and had no way to get home, unless he hitchhiked. And he began to hike late that night, and arrived at the wedding – it was a bitterly cold January day – wearing his suit under his coveralls and carrying his shoes.

The reception was at the house, and as soon as they arrived it became apparent that the furnace was shut off – the oil-tank line was frozen. Ivan put his coveralls back on and went out with a torch and unfroze it, coming back in, his ears raw, and smiling. Thelma, though she remembered this, still pretended she did not.

This pretence persisted when he came in. She pretended she didn't know who he was, and then looked severely at Adele, not for any particular reason except that she had an opportunity to.

"Dontcha member the time I come for the weddin," Ivan said, smiling.

But Thelma, though her eyes registered that she remembered this incident very well, had gone too far in her testament of denial to back down.

"No," she said, smiling the exact same way Adele saw her smile at her when others were present.

Ivan nodded at her in the dark hallway. Then he looked quickly at Adele to show that he knew exactly where he stood.

"Come in, come in," Adele said grouchily, almost as if to protect him by grouchiness. They went into the den, and Thelma, with her back to them, set up her ironing board in the hallway.

The den window faced the southeast and overlooked a field of tangled bushes on the far side of the street. Ralphie and his sister Vera called that the "gully" and they had made a fort there when they were children.

Although the night before Ivan had been very determined to see Adele, he now had nothing to say because Thelma was standing five feet away. He didn't seem to know why he had come, or care about the outcome of it.

And Adele did not want him to talk about Cindi at all because she felt Thelma would get into an argument with him. So every time he mentioned something about it, she would mention something else and then look towards the hallway.

This left Ivan with nothing much to say.

Though Ivan was small of stature, his hands were large and he rested them clumsily on his knees. He had worn his spring jacket and his new pants and shirt. He sat very stiffly on the brick ledge that ran along one side of the den, while Adele sat in the chair with her back to the window – so it looked as if this huge halo had circled her head. And there was something about his tea and how cautiously he tried to drink it. Adele then decided to admonish him to let him know that friendship had limits, and so whenever he said something she found herself disagreeing with it, and looking angrily at him, for the first time in her life. (She, too, knew how he had protected her husband but had suddenly forgotten this.) She was not as skinny as she was as a teenager, but all her movements were the same, which made Ivan look extremely delighted at one moment, and then suddenly frown because she was determined to undercut what he said.

And Adele realized this also. She realized this but couldn't stop – not until he left. After he drove away she became very glum. She walked about the house believing she had betrayed someone, and was not certain who.

After Ivan's visit, Thelma did not speak to her for a month.

"Why is she seeing people like that?" Thelma would ask Vera.

Vera would explain to her the crisis Cindi was now engaged in, which Thelma pretended suddenly not to know anything about.

"Oh my God – oh my God."

Vera would nod in silence.

Thelma, like many of us, often drifted between posture of knowledge or posture of ignorance.

"Those people – drunks and dope addicts – coming into my house and slurping tea."

She told Vera she did not want Adele to have anything to do with that "epileptic" girl. Other reasons could be perceived in her as well, however, by Ralphie who had to listen to a lecture every time he came home. Thelma held him personally responsible for even knowing a man like Ivan.

"Well, we've seen your friends, Ralphie, haven't we – swear words cut into his hands – fine. And Adele likes him, does she – fine. And his wife is having a baby – that retarded girl – just the type to populate the world. Fine, Ralphie. That's the type of people to get to know – of all the good, decent, hardworking, law-abiding people on the river – you drift into the gutter. That's where they come from, Ralphie – just the gutter. People like to always talk about those people as being from here. People even write dirty books about them. So when we go anywhere, it's always those people who've given us a terrible reputation – poachers and murderers and criminals – so we have to lock our doors at night. But you like them – like those people – I see. And I've seen them before, greasy-looking people, you know, with big muscles, always going out of their way to kill somebody. I thought you belonged to the Kinsmen."

Yet underneath he could see that she was glad Adele was involved because it gave her an excuse to be upset. It was in these perverse double standards she was most at home.

For Adele, it wasn't Thelma's abhorrence of sexuality that came through, but a particular type of sexuality.

74

Not the nice discussed sexuality of those who pretended they weren't prudes. And were of course "concerned" about "children." That type of sexuality, the embalmed learned response to the last twenty years, would go right past Adele. But it was the immoral sexuality of a person like Cindi, that brown-headed sexually epileptic, and, worse, of Adele herself that distressed Thelma.

"All having babies and on welfare too – and our taxes supporting the lot of them."

This was one reason why Adele refused to see her child, why she hated most children, and why she believed that Ralphie had betrayed her, because they still lived with his mother.

Whenever Olive and the little girl came, Adele would look out the window, sniff so loud her nose closed completely, and say, "Hum – sure has her dressed funny – gonna look like some little faggoty ballerina." Then she would go up to her room and sit in the corner. Every time she heard the little girl laugh or screech or cry, she would turn up the radio.

"Hey baby baybby-bayyybyyy baby I love you," the music ironically would yelp, drowning out everyone downstairs.

On occasion she would have to see Olive, who dropped in after work. Adele would sit there very politely for about a minute. She knew Olive didn't like her, but she could also tell that Olive knew she was the outcast in the family and no one paid attention to her.

Adele would sit there broodingly quiet and unhappy, scratching a mosquito bite on her foot, or, in defiance, blowing a larger than usual bubble and having it explode over her nose. Then, trying to peel the gum away, she would say, "Hey you?"

"My name's Olive, Adele."

"Right – got any dental floss – or what?"

Olive's face was smooth except for some white hair that sprouted from her chin. And she was a good enough person, Adele supposed, at least that is what she was always telling herself: "Oh, she's a good enough person, I suppose." But in reality every nice thing Olive said only intensified Adele's feeling that she was being left out.

One day Olive made the mistake of mentioning children to Adele. Adele said, "Don't mention them – don't want to know them – hope never to see them. Hope I never have to take care of them. We should abort them all!"

"Is that what you think about Cindi?"

"I don't think nothing about Cindi – I never think about Cindi. Why should I think anything about her?"

Olive looked at her and then looked through her purse for a Kleenex.

"'Cept it seems to me everyone else wants to decide for Cindi – who should be allowed to decide for herself."

"Well," Olive said, "it's just that Cindi is running about now with this cousin of Ruby's from Montreal, and Ruby is worried about her – she's worried that Ivan is going to blow up again."

Adele sniffed and said nothing.

Adele had taken her sneakers off and had rested her feet on the tops of them. Both her feet had black rims about the ankles and both ankles had little red marks on them. She rubbed her feet back and forth to scratch them.

"Well –"

"Ha —"

After a while, Adele left the room.

She went upstairs and walked about in a circle.

No, she didn't like Ruby, she didn't like Cindi, she didn't like Ivan, she detested Ralphie and hated Thelma, and Vera and Nevin were dupes and fools, and the whole lot of them were twits, especially Olive, so there had to be some way to get the child away from her and head to Nova Scotia, or at least to Sussex. And if that didn't come about, she would end up drowning her own daughter, whom she detested the sight of anyway.

And, thinking of this, she headed back down the stairs and marched into the living room, only to find no one there. Then she went into the kitchen.

When she walked in her daughter was sitting on a chair with three big cushions under her, so she could reach the table where the glass of milk was.

"Hello, Dell," the little one said. Then, as always when she saw Adele, her movements became cautious. As if she was used to having Adele pounce on her. The cushions on which she sat seemed to overflow the chair.

She was so tiny her head seemed no bigger than an orange. Her hair was blonde and wispy, as fine as a spiderweb. Her little eyes were black. Her three favourite dolls were sitting in chairs about the table also, each of them on cushions as well. She wore one red sock, the other was in the far corner of the kitchen, lying heel up near the stove. When Adele saw this, she stopped and looked about as if confused. Her face changed.

"Where Walphie?" the child said.

"There," Adele said. "You have to have every cushion in the house down in the kitchen though, don't you? And the arm of Snoopy is torn off again – I noticed that right away!"

With this, Adele smiled. The little girl stopped smiling and reached clumsily for her milk.

Everything was Vera nowadays. The family revolved around her now. Vera was practical-minded. Vera gave piano lessons to little "underprivileged" children from Barryville. Vera belonged to "concerned and forward thinking" women's rights organizations. Vera was going to have her child at home – in her own bedroom and not in some "sterilized foreign" atmosphere created by the hospital.

All of this had Dr. Hennessey upset, but Vera had gone instead to Dr. Savard, who said it was a perfectly reasonable thing to wish. That is, she wanted a midwife. This idea for Thelma was "new and fresh." And Vera was something of a saint for being as she was.

Unfortunately Vera didn't remember that Hennessey had helped deliver children all over the river – from a wagon to a half-ton truck. That old Mrs. Garrett's children had all been born in the bed where they were conceived, and it was not such a strikingly new idea at all. What was new was only the attitude developed because of other criteria, and Hennessey was worried because of Vera's health, which had been so bad a few years ago.

But, in fact, Hennessey was looked upon as old-fashioned and out of touch, and, of course, a woman-hater, while Savard was looked upon as a person who understood the problems of modern society and was willing to challenge them – all because of a birth at home, of which Hennessey had done over a hundred and Savard had not yet done one. Also, Vera went about mentioning words like "birthing." It was "birthing" this and "birthing" that with Vera. The old doctor visited, took her blood pressure, weight, and checked for too much fluid. But the doctor, though he disliked the idea, realized that she was set on it.

As far as Adele was concerned, this made the baby-to-be a rather political baby-to-be, and not just an ordinary baby like hers was – which was born in the men's washroom of the community centre. But Vera was adamant about this, and her health wasn't good.

Adele, of course, hated the whole idea of Vera's pregnancy, of her going to have the child at home – or what she hated was the climate about the two opposing pregnancies. Vera was not supposed to get pregnant, but she did – and now it was absolutely natural that she did. Cindi, everyone perceived, could get pregnant every time she dropped her pants, and this was absolutely unnatural. Olive was "expert" at "mothering," as Adele was told, while Adele, who had the child, was never mentioned as a mother.

Savard, who spent most of his time at the beach in the summer, drank wine until they held up a towel so he could get sick, and always had young girls around him, always looked sad at just the right time, was wonderful, according to some, while Dr. Hennessey, now in his seventies, who had refused to go to beaches no matter how many times he was invited, and imbibed only by himself, who never got sentimental, was the fellow whose opinion was least likely to be sought.

As for Ivan himself, he didn't understand very much of this. He did not know why Vera and Nevin dressed like Mennonites, lived on a farm they knew nothing about, had a tractor that they could not fix, and did not work in town – like everyone else here, who lived down river.

He did not understand why they were so easily duped, why Antony felt it was his obligation to cheat them – not once but many times – and why, of all the people on the river, they clung to him. Why they wanted horses that they didn't understand, and why they had chickens which were unmannered enough to sit on the kitchen table while Vera and Nevin ate.

He did not understand why they went to university and got degrees – Vera had her Master's in English and Nevin had a B.A. and B.Ed. – and then refused to work at jobs their degrees might entitle them to. He did not know them very well, and he always considered educated people better than he was.

He saw them disdain being employed and only now, because Vera was pregnant, were they trying to recoup their losses, were they trying to get back this prosperity they might have if they decided to work at jobs they would have been suited for.

And since he loved Ralphie he would not say anything about them.

He did not understand this.

Ivan was a little wary of educated people. Not, of course, all the time, but if he had to take his sister down to Dr. Savard, as he did one afternoon, he found himself tongue-tied and shy, and fighting not to be. He found himself shy in front of Vera, the only time he met her. He did not understand Nevin, but he would not allow anyone to make fun of him while he was there.

Ivan felt unequal to words and writing, to books and knowledge of that kind, but he had a tremendous respect for it. In such ways he was left out of life, not because he had to be, but simply because he was.

Once Ralphie gave him a book that was written by one of the local writers. Ralphie told him he might like it.

In the end, he thought Ralphie was making fun of him. Why would a writer put swearing in a book, he'd asked Ralphie. He felt a book was sacred – even though he never read one – and you didn't put swear words into it. He did not understand why Ralphie thought he would like that book. Secretly he felt it was because he himself cursed and would therefore never understand a book that didn't have those words.

He never mentioned the book again. But since Ralphie had given it to him he lugged it everywhere. He had it in Port Hawkesbury when he worked there, and now he had it set up on the old greasy shelf in the cuddy.

He did not know why Vera wanted a midwife and why she wanted to have her child at home. But there must be a reason for it. For instance, he reflected, an aunt of his had to lie still for the last three months of her pregnancy in the summer heat. For Ivan, it had to be something like this.

So he asked his grandmother to go over and visit Vera sometimes if she could, and to sit with her.

He did not know what else to do about that situation, but he was proud he had thought of this. That'll fix things for her, he thought.

And he was happy about this.

But there was not much else to be happy about. He

heard that Cindi and some people were going to the Island together, to party, and he knew she was drinking.

He resolved finally to do something about it.

He went to see her, and took his sleeping bag. He walked in, set it down, and asked her if she could mend it.

There were two other people in the apartment whom he didn't know. It was strange to have them in his apartment. The oak cabinet and the smell of onions, the wobbly bar stools. He did not ask who they were either. One seemed to be a friend of Dorval Gene's.

He had the appearance of a man who had tanned himself under a light, and he looked at Ivan with the self-assured look strangers give when they feel they've been informed about you. Ivan, for the most part, ignored them.

"Could you sew this up," Ivan said. He did not look at her but at the tanned blond man in the summer shirt with the wristband on.

"No – I'm sorry," she said.

"You – you can't," he said.

"No," she said. She stared straight ahead.

They both knew that, far from being anything else, this was his plea for clemency.

He picked the sleeping bag up and walked towards the door.

"Okay, never mind, I'll do it!" she said.

He kept walking towards the door.

"Okay, never mind, I'll do it, I said."

"Never mind," Ivan said, "I won't bother you no more."

"You hurt my feelings," he heard her say. "I spose ya don't know that, for, do ya!"

He left the apartment, smelling the smell of oil and salt in the hot, carpeted hallway.

It was a muggy day, filled with blackflies. The foliage was heavy and drooped green. Now and then the sun would just break out and then be encompassed in haze.

The woods was as silent as if it was waiting for a forest fire.

II

II

7

The tavern was hot, and a slack heat came under the window, propped open with a stick, and Antony sat with his back to this heat, breathing uniformly, his mouth closed, his shirt undone so that the top of his white undershirt, which he'd put on backwards that morning, was visible, tag and all. He looked at Eugene who was sitting beside him. They had been talking for an hour or more. It was now some time after four in the afternoon, just past the hottest point of the day, when wisps of heat drove across the naked parking lot, and the drive-in screen in the distance, past the waving maples, looked like some monstrosity.

Eugene was from Montreal, so he was called Dorval Gene. Everyone laughed at his mistakes and playfully dismissed them. Once he sent the grader all the way to Point Sapin for no reason, and he neglected to report the front-end loader was down – he upset three one-hundred-pound propane tanks – any of which would have caused trouble for him if it was not for the fact he was Clay's sister's son.

Eugene, like many people from large cities, grew up without much understanding of the outside world. He wore loose summer shirts, and black pants with black pointed shoes. He had a huge double chin. He had thick glasses that made his left ear pinch out, and people were conscious of him saying things, which he might have felt were cosmopolitan but which he knew didn't fit him as a person, and allowed the nickname Dorval Gene to have more poignancy.

Everything was quiet and had been for a while. Gordon Russell had come and gone with his instructions to take the pinball machines out of the mini-mart and take them across the river to the new Nite Owl, and he had left these instructions while Antony was only half aware of the man's presence. Antony was more concerned with Eugene, who was here for vacation, and therefore special. And a person whom Ruby wanted Cindi to get together with.

"He hauled a knife on you and everything," Antony said. "That's the worst of it – it has Nannie crying her eyes out."

Eugene said nothing. Heat came through the tavern door and some Indian boys from Burnt Church had come in with a young woman – a half-breed whom Antony had seen over the last few years. Her hair was dyed bright orange and her lacklustre skin was dotted nutmeg about the cheeks.

"Yes – he hauled a knife – he was always that kind. If you want my opinion, the reason Gloria and I are separated is because of him," he whispered shyly. "Always out attacking people – and Gloria at home crying." He paused and drank and looked about. "It came down to either me going with Gloria" – he hesitated – "or to stay with Ivan, who was already a mittful back then. Well, you've heard it yerself by now."

He took another drink, moved his chair out, and looked at his boots as he tapped them. He spoke so quietly Eugene could hardly hear him.

"Gloria says, 'Wash yer hands of him,' and I said, 'How can I – he's my flesh and blood.'" He looked up at Eugene and grabbed his arm, with tears in his eyes. "Like having to run up to Shelby's to get him to come home at twelve o'clock at night, and him blind drunk at nine years old" – he reached for his second draft – "stealin marbles – plumbers – from the Savoy kid." Antony said this and then scratched his nose quickly and drank.

"It was a hard time then," Eugene said, looking at him with sincerity and sympathy.

"Well, he took the life right out of my wife," Antony whispered. "You know yerself about Gloria, and I don't need to tell you about Gloria. It's hard for me to do – I think of all the people who put Gloria down," he said. "You know something, she herself never says a peep about anyone." He finished his draught and ordered another. "All the talk about Ivan and Cindi, well you know yerself what they say, and I don't go on about it, but she wouldn't be pregnant if he didn't force her to stop taking her birth control."

Antony was angry with Ivan today.

Ivan had come out of the woods, where he had been peeling pulp, and they'd just had an argument. The week before Antony had sold some goats to Nevin and Vera. Vera was too tired to argue, and Nevin was always easily talked into things. It was about eighty degrees at noon hour. Vera listened to Nevin plead to her about these goats, while Antony stood in the living room with his hat in his hand. Vera finally went: "Whew – okay – okay – some hot." She smiled at Nevin as Nevin hugged her and then took a deep breath.

Now the goats walked in and out of the house anytime, day or night – and unfortunately Nevin was frightened of them.

Ivan was upset about the goats. He threw his boots against the wall and sat on the couch.

"Don't blame me," Antony said. "No one's gonna take a goat unless they want to, so why blame me for that?" Antony looked at his son. He looked particularly put out at this moment, as if he had always had the best intentions – and was now all at once reconciled to being misunderstood by everyone.

"Is Nannie down there?" Ivan said. "Vera needed some help."

Antony shook his head. "No, she isn't," he said.

"Why not?"

"I can't have an old woman going down and sitting in that heat. I don't know what's wrong with that place – freeze in the winter – there's a gale force right in the living room, blows a match out at twenty feet, and in the summer you sweat yer bag off just saying hello to them. Back-to-the-landers all right – I wish the Christ they would go away. But – it's me they call up to go down and see about their topsoil – who was it they asked to go down and see about their topsoil, Ivan?"

After this, Ivan said nothing else and Antony was free to tell him all that he had done for Vera and Nevin – which was considerably more than Clay Everette Madgill, the person he often used as a yardstick. "Clay never likes new ideas," he said.

After this conversation Antony went to the tavern where he met Eugene, eating a pepper steak.

Of course Eugene had no idea that he would be so involved, but he was staying at his uncle's, Clay Madgill's, and like a lot of visitors to the Maritimes he was captivated and surprised by the vitality and perception of the people, and their often careless attitude.

When Ivan was in the woods, Eugene and Ruby had helped Cindi leave the apartment. Eugene had taken her from the apartment, carried her suitcase to the car, and fidgeted when Cindi went back in to water the plants, and then came down the stairs carrying a huge plant in a pot. Then they all got into the car, and, with Eugene driving, smoking a small cigar with the tip gone yellow with smoke, with the leaves of the plant sticking out the window, they went down the road.

No one knew where she was, and this bothered Antony.

"No one should tell anyone where she is," he said.

Eugene had an urge to tell him where she was. He would look at his plate and fight the urge to speak.

"Poor little Cindi," Antony said.

Eugene nodded but still kept his eyes on his plate.

"Well, she's in a good place now – I suppose."

"Yes she is," Eugene said, and he spoke as if he suddenly knew all the particulars of Cindi's unfortunate life – which all of them, being concerned, could describe as unfortunate. "No one'll hurt her again," Eugene said.

"Well," Antony said, "it's better that way, I suppose – the fewer knows the better."

Eugene thought for a moment.

"Well, if something happens, we can always get the message to her – you know what I mean."

"Oh, for sure – for sure," Antony said. "For sure," he said again.

Then he yawned and looked bored. Out the tavern window the heat was like a drizzle, the clumps of weed at the far end of the gravelled parking lot were matted with dust, the wires stung, and beyond that the sky was immeasurably blue and cloudless.

Ivan used to walk down this highway collecting bottles in the summer in a pair of grey shorts, Antony recalled.

He had a bag of songs written by the time he was sixteen – and he played a guitar, though it only had four strings. "Pining for You in Pineville" and "Desperato Kid," and one which he could never sing on the river without getting into trouble was called "Why Bigtooled Darlins Fight." There were songs called "Newcastle June" and "My Chatham Park." He wrote songs about Loggieville and Burnt Church, Bartibog and as far upriver as Storeytown.

When he was young, Gloria dressed him in cowboy boots and a small rhinestone blazer, with a cowboy hat with a feather, and took him to Dominion Day celebrations to sing, and people used to get him to sign their programs because he was famous. Then they would all go for ice cream. And Gloria had red lipstick, and Antony said she was so beautiful he cried, and they all laughed and bought Nannie a present.

Now, as Antony looked out the window, he caught sight of a young Indian boy carrying a sack full of bottles in the ditch.

The Indian woman with the orange hair and nutmeg cheeks looked in his direction, noticed his undershirt was on backwards, and laughed, holding her golden beer up to her lips.

After a while, knowing Eugene wouldn't tell him anything, Antony left the tavern. He crossed the road – his truck was parked on the other side of the highway. There was a smell of stingers in the afternoon, and the scent of spruce gum also. When he got home the house was empty. The door creaked on its hinges.

Margaret had just finished her last exam. She had put on her shorts and was sitting behind the house. The horse, Rudolf, was in the small paddock on her left. There was the sound of the little spring that ran from their property down to Vera and Nevin's. When he came out on the porch steps he stood and looked down at her. She didn't look his way.

"Where is everyone – where's Val?" he said.

"She went out to supper."

"Out to supper – out to supper – out to supper with who –"

"Nannie and Grampie."

"Nannie and Grampie – ha – what for?"

"I don't know – because she finished school – they all went out to the mall – Nannie and Grampie and Valerie," she said.

She glanced up at him out of the corner of her eye, and then back down towards Vera's place. The back of Vera's house was in bright sunshine but the windows were closed – it looked and even had the presence of an invalid's house, with the sun shining on its white side and one rag on the line.

"Well, isn't that something – out for supper," he said. "Out for supper – why didn't you go?"

"I didn't want to go."

"Why not –"

"I didn't want to."

Antony licked his sapphire ring and took it off, and then he pulled his knuckle. There was a small snap. Then he lit a cigarette. He looked at his daughter in her pink shorts and with her thighs very white in the late-afternoon sunshine, with the smell of wet grass under the porch.

"I don't want you going out later either," he said suddenly.

"I'm not going anywhere –"

"No," he said, confused. "Well, are you going to make me some supper?"

"What do you want?" she asked.

"What do I want – ha – I have to take those pinball machines across the river. What do you think – I want some supper," he said.

She looked at him as she always did, and then got up and went inside. The bottom of her shorts were covered in tar.

"You've been down at the wharf," he said, "with those lads."

"I have not," she snapped, and ran in and slammed the screen door.

Antony then walked down the path towards Vera's. At the point where he usually saw the bird's nest, he stopped and looked about. Ivan pulled into the yard and got out of the car. Antony stayed where he was for a moment. Then he walked back up the hill, and came out by the shed. There was the smell of wood and torn tar paper.

"Where's Cindi?" Ivan asked.

Antony took a breath.

"That's what I been trying to find out for you," he said.

Ivan said nothing. He had just come from the woods. He was covered in sweat. His body looked healthier at this moment than it had in some time.

"I went to the apartment and she's gone," Ivan said.

"Of course she is! What in hell do you think I've been trying to tell you? And I been down river all day trying to get some information – about where she's gone," his father said.

"Well," Ivan said calmly, "where is she?"

"Gone – how the hell should I know. Oh, she's got important friends now – she couldn't give a fuck for her husband. That guy from Montreal there – Eugene – just the same as I went through, you wait and see. I'm going in to have supper – big-feelinged Nannie went out to the mall to eat – come on and we'll have some supper."

And with that he picked up a stick, took a look over his shoulder, went back to make sure the lock on the shed was snapped, and, whistling, he went into the house, a cloud of moths about his head. Ivan followed him, not knowing what there was to whistle about.

Margaret had tried to fry some hamburgers and had blackened them. Antony was sitting at the table, bent over, staring through his hands at his boots and tapping his feet, waiting for his supper. The more he tapped his feet and whistled, the more nervous Margaret became. Instead of turning the heat on the stove lower, she turned it higher and went into the other room to put on an album that she had saved her money for.

Grease spattered against the side of the walls, and smoke filled the room. Antony looked at the stove and shook his head, and Ivan went over and turned the heat down and took the pan off the burner.

"Christ," Margaret said coming in, looking at her father quickly and then at Ivan.

"It's all right," Ivan said, "I got it."

Margaret was at that age that some girls never reach. When she talked she sounded thirteen, she was fifteen and looked nineteen. Her feet were bare, yet her fingernails were long and painted and her breasts well formed. Upstairs she kept scrapbooks, and drew pictures of dogs and cows and coloured them, and had the names of boys written over her schoolbooks.

"What in hell are you doing?" Antony said. "You'll burn the house down."

Ivan looked at his father calmly and then at Margaret, who was nervously trying to pick the hamburgers up with a spatula, and said: "It's all right – here."

He told Margaret to go and sit at the table.

"But the soup," she said, in French, "the soup is boiling."

Ivan answered her in French that he would get the soup and moved carefully around her, not because of her, but because he didn't want to upset Antony, who was licking his sapphire ring in order to put it back on.

It was after supper. A breeze had come up, and the trees across the road and along the dirt lane to Vera's were waving, while the sky was filled with gold. On the chair in her room, by the window, Margaret sat painting her toenails while her brother Ivan, his shirt tied in a knot against his belly, and his belly as taut as a young welterweight, with his sleeves rolled up to his elbows, watched her.

He spoke to her in *franglais* – that mixture of French and English – that the French along the roadway spoke one another. Margaret wanted to be a veterinarian. She loved goats and ducks. In fact, she drew pictures of ducks and put them all over her room, and she had ducks on two of her T-shirts.

"I just wonder," Margaret said pensively, and trying to sound very grown-up suddenly, but sounding more like a thirteen-year-old than the nineteen-year-old, "will Cindi come down to visit me?"

"For sure she will," Ivan said. When he spoke he tried to sound as if everything had come to a conclusion that he himself had favoured.

Margaret looked at him out of the corner of her eye, while adjusting the Kleenex between her toes.

"I don't know why she would leave you anyways," Margaret said.

"Well, I have nothing to say about it."

"Dad told Nannie you batted her about and kicked her – in the guts."

"Ya, well Dad should take care of Dad," Ivan said. Then he butted his cigarette after two drags.

After she adjusted the Kleenex between her toes, Margaret walked on her heels to the door and closed it.

"Everyone knows where she is anyways," Margaret said.

"Where?" Ivan said. "Where in fuck is she?"

Then, as always, when she tried to sound as grown-up as she looked, she managed to be childlike.

"Everyone knows – it's where Ruby goes." Although, at that moment, she didn't seem to be quite sure of herself.

"Ruby goes where?"

"Well, that apartment down river."

Yet before she could speak any more, say another word, Ivan had left the room.

Ivan decided he couldn't go there. And that's where Antony had the advantage over him. Not that Antony was waiting for an advantage – he, like all of us, never knew one moment what was going to happen the next – but he happened to be in his room and overheard most of the conversation. He could hear it as clearly as if he were in Margaret's room itself. He waited until Ivan left, then he stood up and walked along the hallway heavily. The window at the end of the hallway was spotted and showed the back field. There was some yellow weed in the sun. Far away the bay was spotless, and he remembered swimming when he was a boy, and how they would all run through the stubbled hay field to get the cows to lick the salt off their skin, and then lay down against the hay bale and watch the blue sky above them while they ate licorice from the store. When he was fifteen he went to work for his uncle.

He walked into Margaret's room. She had her small fan going and was drying her toes as she leaned back against a chair. She had taken Ivan's cigarette out of the ashtray and had it lit – and though it had a hole in it where some tobacco seeped through, she was puffing dramatically on it, completely oblivious to her father's presence.

"Now you went and told him everything," Antony said, as if he'd known Cindi's whereabouts all along.

Margaret sat up so quickly she almost caught one of her toes in the fan, and flipped the cigarette under her sweater.

"I don't care," she said. "He should know where Cindi is."

"Yes, so he can put her through the same misery your mother put me through," Antony said, "and beat her up again. He's a dangerous man – that lad."

"He will not," Margaret said. "And Cindi is spose to come down and visit me too."

"Well, she won't come down and visit ya because she doesn't like ya – she never liked you, matter-of-fact."

Margaret became solemn and stone-faced.

"I'm sending you to a boarding school and a convent and let the nuns take care of you – and don't think they won't whip you into shape," he said, coming to stand over her.

Margaret said nothing. She remained very stone-faced, while smoke seeped through the neck and short sleeves of her white sweater.

"I have a lot to do tonight," Antony said. "I can't go way down river and look out for her."

His forehead and the hair on his head was damp. He was sure of only one thing – that it was his responsibility (and he could later relate this responsibility to Gloria).

"Well," she said to him in French, "you always take everyone else's side but your own family's."

He was stunned that she would say this to him, and yet as soon as she said it he felt that this was the one remark he had been anticipating from her for a long time.

And he looked the way Ivan had often seen him look – genuinely sad and confused. He made a shadow against the blowing curtain.

"I don't know what kind of toe polish yer using," he said, "but it smells like burnt shirts or something – I can't get a handle on it. And another thing," he said loudly, as he always spoke loudly when he was nervous, "I don't know when girls grow up – how long it takes to make all their parts the right appearance, but," he said, stammering, "be careful of yer shorts."

She said nothing but looked mortified, and he, too, looked embarrassed.

"And," he concluded, as if to negate what he had just said, "I'm taking one of yer ducks over to Val's room – she should have a duck too. I never understood why you should have all the ducks."

And with that he picked up a large ceramic duck that Vera had made Margaret and went out of the room. Margaret stood and began to slap herself frantically, as if to put herself out.

8

Two hours later, almost dead drunk, Antony was at the apartment, sitting in a big chair.

There was no food in the apartment as yet. Cindi had found some soda crackers and she drank water, with her big potted plant sitting on the waxed floor near the rolled-up rug. She had gotten twenty-five bags of tea.

There was no television in the apartment either. So Cindi sat in the chair in the corner, her eyes squinted shut and her feet tapping. Since she was a TV addict, this was driving her crazy. The telephone hadn't been installed. The apartment had the look and feel of emptiness – which was saturated with a June heat wave. But people did come and go, day and night – like they do under certain conditions in dormitories or residences, or late-night places of business.

Antony, in fact, had arrived just like this. Bop, and he was there – with his friend Ernie. Ernie was staring at Cindi in the most peculiar way any man had ever stared at her. He looked at her as if he had never seen her before. He had worn his best pair of jeans. And whenever she looked at him he would nod urgently. He shook her hand three times, until, when he looked her way, she hid her hand behind her back.

"Momma don't even know where I am," he said. He looked at Ruby and smiled. He seemed to consider this a very bad place to be. It seemed that he wanted to tell them that he knew he shouldn't be here, but soon, overcome with drink and sleep, he curled up in a corner and slept, infrequently letting out a cry and kicking his feet and punching.

Cindi felt frightened of this behaviour. But the most important thing for Cindi, as her mother – who looked and had the work done to look like an older Gina Lollobrigida – had taught her, was manners. And manners Cindi had. Because she clung to them as a device to save herself from all the wise people that she came into contact with. She was always polite and nice, and tried to be attractive. She never swore in her life. Her mother had told her that if she swore her mouth would fill up with dirt – and even when others said a dirty word, she would clamp her mouth shut. This is why Cindi had always fallen for older men – like Gordon Russell. Gordon never swore in front of her. He was married and he had left her in a motel on the Island three years ago, in fact, stranded her (like other men had), but he had never sworn at her or in her presence.

He was not that old either – only forty at the time they "loved" each other. She had been nineteen.

"It's just because he has a wife, huh," she said to Ruby.

"That's probably it," Ruby said.

"Oh, wow," Cindi said, and she smiled.

Cindi had had a child by Gordon, which he had told her wasn't his – and he looked so hurt that he broke up with her. He was hurt that it wasn't his child, and Cindi, as always when people looked at her, had lowered her eyes.

"I think it is – if you don't know," she said. And she said this in a peevish little singsong voice.

"It's not my child – I can't have children," Gordon had said.

"You – can't?"

"No, dear – that's the one thing I have learned – unfortunately. It breaks my heart."

"I thought you had children," Cindi said, in the same singsong voice.

"My wife can have children," Gordon said. He sat on the side of the bed, in the smell of the soiled clothes and sneakers, with suntan lotion over his skin. He sat with his head down, at the Seaview Motel, and Cindi sat with her eyes half-closed and her fingers clasped together.

"My wife has the children," he said. "I mean – we adopted them – my wife loves children – my wife's a good-hearted woman. I don't want you thinking you're better than she is," he said, suddenly shaking his fist at her. He was shaking all over. He looked like he was going to cry.

Cindi said nothing. Lots of men had shaken their fists at her. But then he left her there. He started to cry about his wife and then he got mad at her.

Cindi went home, and for seven months she sat in the clapboard house near the trailer park with her mother. She had had two children now. Her sister kept one – she lived with an RCMP officer in Buctouche. Her mother kept the second child.

103

Ruby walked from the door to the window, looked out the window and then walked back to the door. Cindi watched her walking. Then, with nothing else to do, she whistled into the top of a pop bottle and tapped her feet. In fact, she was enjoying herself doing this. But she looked up to notice Ruby glaring at her. Then bravely she gave the bottle one final toot, and slowly lowered it and cleared her throat.

Antony was in a "blackout." He started saying he was bringing a lawsuit against his father because he owned one-eighth of the Chevrolet engine in his father's boat.

"He never takes that into consideration when he's out gaffing onto lobster traps," Antony said suddenly. "But he takes Vally and Nannie out for a big dinner at the mall." Then he looked at Cindi blankly, as if wondering why she was here on such a beautiful night.

Every now and again Antony would look over towards Ernie, who was asleep, and give him a kick. "No – he never does," he continued speaking. "He should be building me a house, Ruby – like yer father is building for you – but I never got a house – Gloria can tell you – I never got one house outta that cocksucker. Well anyways, I'm through with being Mr. Niceguy – fixing his driveway that time and paying his taxes."

Then he sighed and looked about.

Antony had come here in a hurry after drinking a bottle or two of Hermit. Now here he was. Why, it was hard to say. Perhaps he wanted to warn them about Ivan coming, but, at any rate, Antony was caught up with this. Antony, when drinking, often got on a train of thought and couldn't get off it, or he found something going on and he had to be involved in it. It didn't matter what it was – bingo at the centre three summers ago – Antony had to try and run it. And when they were making MacDonald Farm a historical property, Antony had to be there as well – as a matter of fact, he was there every day, right from the moment they were beginning to clear out all the old bricks and rubble until they kicked him off the property for trying to sell a stuffed beaver to the tourists.

He was hoping he would be able to show everyone how much he was doing – but even this was too definite. It was more that he was here instead of staying at home. He had taken Margaret's duck and put it in Val's room. He was still thinking of the fill that he had to get for Dr. Hennessey. He was back and forth instead of staying put.

Something happens, and you think you are the one making it happen – that if you decide to go somewhere, you are reasonable enough to understand why, and so on. But the people in this room were a perfect example that this was not the way things happened to anyone. Ruby would not have been involved except it was the way she spent all her summers. For Ruby, all her summers contained the same things. Excitement and bravado, and usually at someone else's expense.

Last year it was one of her father's workers. He had cancer, and Ruby, who had never lacked good-heartedness, spent the whole summer taking him back and forth to Halifax for treatment. She organized a party for him and did what she could, always slightly conscious that she, beautiful and vital and alive, had taken over the centre from his own family, who at the end resented her.

Secretly Ruby had not felt close to Cindi in the last few years. They had drifted apart. In fact, until this happened, she felt Cindi was a bother, and hardly visited. Now that she had become Cindi's guardian she was also responsible for her, and found all the dislike she had had for Cindi every time they got at close quarters together.

For a long while Antony had them worried that Ivan would come. At every sound Antony would turn his head. "What the hell is that – listen."

"Jesus, Antony, ya got us all nervous as a cat," Ruby said.

"Cindi, you can come out of the bathroom – he's not here."

And Cindi would come out of the bathroom and sit near the window.

"Dangerous lad," Antony said, "dangerous lad, that!"

❖ ❖ ❖

That night there was one of those impromptu parties that happen so often in the summer. People, knowing Ruby had rented an apartment, dropped in. Lionel was there. And Oniseme walked in and sat down for a moment. Then Gordon Russell came in. They brought beer and wine and rum.

Often Ruby would disappear for whole minutes at a time, leaving Cindi alone with six or seven men. Cindi would look out and see her in the phone booth down the street. She was telephoning her boyfriend in town. Only Cindi knew this other aspect of Ruby's summer. Like a bird forced to fly in the dark, Ruby zigzagged.

The party opened up, and things were said. And like parties on the river, everything could foul up at any second.

"I'm scared Eugene is so involved in this here racket," Antony said suddenly. "I mean, I know how he is just visiting here – it gives him a bad impression of us, and sorta a bad impression of my family." He wanted this statement to have a very good impression on them.

He looked over at Cindi for a second, and then looked towards Gordon, who nodded. Gordon already had put his arm around Cindi. Cindi, who always loved people to hug her, felt that because they used to go together he could take this liberty. It added piquancy. And so Cindi started to cry.

"I know," Cindi said, "I know – I'm sorry, I'm sorry." She kept saying that, for ten minutes. Her shorts were very loose, and the men, some of them trying not to, could not help staring up her legs – for everything was visible there.

"That's what I told Eugene today," Antony said in a heavy voice. "'I don't want to know where she is,' I said, 'I don't want to know a thing about it – because Ivan's certain to find out.' I had enough trouble with that young fucker already," Antony said, tears coming to his eyes as they often did when he drank.

Cindi suddenly lit a cigarette, and looked scared, and Gordon gave her another hug.

"But I told him, 'Gordon, you wait until Cindi finds another man – a man who knows the value of a woman, and everything about a woman.'"

"I'm sorry," Cindi said, in that peevish singsong voice she had when she was accused of something, or when people told her she was lying.

"And then Margaret went and said to me tonight, 'Dad, ya always loved yer own,'" Antony said, conscious that people were listening to him because he was talking about Ivan, and conscious and irritable that he was attacking his own again, in front of people, just like Margaret said he would, and couldn't seem to stop.

"Loved yer own?" Oniseme said.

"Loved yer own – that's what she said, loved yer own. 'Why now do you turn against Ivan,' and I just said to Margaret, 'Listen here – just a minute'" – he said this very loud, so everyone looked at him – "I loved my own till it hurt. I sacrificed my marriage, and went to the hospital, but Cindi is my own also – and Ivan is my own too – but do I hurt a hair's breath on yer heads or do I fly off the handle?'

"'No Daddy,' she said to me, crying ya know – crying like that all, crying 'no Daddy, I just want to know.' And so I said, 'Well – how can I love Ivan the less if I love Cindi the more?'"

"I don't know," some people said.

"I sure don't know either, eh," Antony said. Then he asked if there was any tea in the house, and looked towards the cupboards.

"I bought some tea," Cindi said. "I'll make you some."

She stood and went to the cupboard. Since her pregnancy her feet had started to swell, but Gordon didn't know why. He simply looked at them and said:

"What's wrong with yer feet?"

Cindi turned, with a dreamy expression, and looked down at them.

"Feet bigger than Harold Matchett, if you ask me," Gordon said. Then he laughed that coarse, unpleasant laugh, which was loud and always tried to bring attention to himself, something that Antony could never like.

And Cindi laughed too.

Ruby came back in and sat down near Oniseme. Two other men came in with her. A huge grey moth with a succulent body and lots of powder batted itself haplessly against a light. The place was filled with smoke, the smell of smoked oysters and beer.

Cindi had promised herself that she was not going to drink, but the man Ivan had seen in the apartment with her, the man who had the band on his wrist, made her a rum daiquiri.

Up until now, Antony felt he had spoken too much, and had said all the foolish things that he always seemed to say in front of people he wanted to respect him. But he wanted to redeem himself. He wanted to hit someone, to make people go away. He knew three or four of the men had gone into the kitchen with Cindi, and this bothered him for some reason.

"Oh wow," he heard Cindi saying.

He knew that if Ivan were here they wouldn't dare do such a thing. He was overcome thinking of little Margaret and her ducks, and how she was saving her money for the Exhibition – and how innocent that seemed compared to this.

"Tell us how the ram went at Nevin," Ruby said, looking at him, and kicking him on the knee, as if she understood that he was upset. Ruby could read people very well, and she tried to get him back into a good mood.

"Who me?"

"Yes – tell me – I heard it last time I just about fell down and pissed my pants."

Antony looked at everyone.

"Well, animals of any sort have to respect you or they'll take advantage of you," Antony said, lighting a

109

cigarette and looking at the match for a second. "So many people don't know the psychology of an animal." He blew the match out. "The first thing you do in front of a horse is kill a chicken – then that horse will never kick you in the head or bite your ear off." He looked at them suspiciously for some reason. "I had a dog – you know, Muffins. I had to kick the shit out of it, or it would have torn my throat out. It never learned till the day it ran away – kept trying to attack me. I tried to get it to attack other people, but it wouldn't. Jesus, it wasn't a big dog either – no bigger than a fox really. So every day I'd grab it by the scruff of the neck and kick it . . . boot it . . . and hide its dog dish – and everything else – and still it kept coming back for more." Here he paused knowing he had gone off track. "But let me tell you – those goats down at Nevin's are having the time of their lives, because they take one look at Nevin and go right at him, chase him all over the lawn, and him scared. And then Margaret – you know Margaret, my oldest girl, going in to be a veterinarian in two years there at the university – she just had to go down and handle those goats for him and catch his rabbits – which he is continually mixing up, the males and females, so there is more and more rabbits popping up everywhere. It's a circus down there," he said, with that particular self-righteousness he had whenever he finished a statement.

"Well," Ruby said, disappointed, "it's not the same way as you told it before – but it's still okay."

Everyone laughed, and Antony laughed too.

Everyone was silent for a moment, and then some friend of Dorval Gene's, the tanned youngster with the wristband, began to laugh hysterically over something in Antony's story. And Antony felt stung. He looked at Ruby, as if for some approval or reassurance, but she paid no attention to him.

"You," he said to Cindi, suddenly and angrily, "have got to get your life together."

"I am," Cindi said.

"Ha – you are," Antony said, sniffing. "I bet you are."

"I'm sorry," Cindi said. "I'm sorry like I toldja all before – I toldja last week and everything." And she put her head down and wouldn't lift it.

"Leave her alone now," Gordon said, "for Godsakes, Antony."

"Oh, I'm not saying anything to her," Antony smiled weakly.

Gordon looked at him, in the disappointed fashion a more wordly and clever man can do, and Antony said:

"Hell, I'm just jokin" – and he felt his face sting. "Aren't I, Cindi – I'm just jokin, dear – just jokin – ya know that."

"Yes," Cindi said, head still down. "Antony is always coming to visit me." She spoke into her sweater, so they could hardly understand what she said.

"Oh, Cindi dear," Ruby said, and real tears flooded her eyes. Her face looked almost more beautiful when she cried.

"I don't think we should be too hard on Ivan," Lionel said suddenly. "I mean, he just made a mistake – all of this has been going on now for over a long time. I know Ivan – he helped me rig up a switch to bypass to my starter. Never charged me nothin."

"The hell with Ivan," Antony said suddenly. He looked about and grabbed himself a beer, opened it and drank.

Cindi, however, still kept her head low, breathing peevishly into her sweater.

"I know lots about Ivan," Antony said. "Lots and lots, but I'm not blaming anybody. Everyone thinks I'm blaming people. I could tell you about a party at Ivan's and Cindi's, Ruby. Let me tell you," he said. "Remember, Cindi? I come in in the morning and here a woman is on the couch with Ivan –"

Cindi knew that this had happened in an innocent way, that she had had a seizure the night before, and Brenda Gulliver was down there because of that. That Ivan, so he wouldn't disturb her, fell asleep sitting on the couch where Brenda was lying. But Cindi couldn't lift her head to speak. She only nodded and fumbled with her fingers.

Antony nodded his head and looked about, as if he had proven something. Falsehood doesn't care whether it is false or not, but dares people to expose it as such. The young men only laughed again.

And suddenly the rage of the whole afternoon's drinking, of Margaret, of Val going out for dinner, of Gordon being there, overcame him.

He jumped up and grabbed Lionel and hit him twice on the top of the head.

"Don't you dare mention Ivan to me. I put up, and Gordon knows – Gordon knows – Gordon knows."

Everyone jumped up to stop what was happening. There was some pushing.

"For Godsakes, settle down," Ruby said, "or get the Jesus out."

Lionel tried to cover his head.

"Gordon knows I put pinball machines on this river – Gordon knows –"

Then Cindi walked by them, went along the hallway, and had a seizure. She fell over with a thud and landed on her side, blinking and in convulsions, near her plotted plant.

9

Ivan did not hear about the seizure. He didn't go to the apartment. The next morning he had to return two bridles to his grandfather's, and it was here he met Antony.

Antony was in his father's shed, trying to find a bucket for Nevin and Vera. He had promised them a bucket the week before, and had not got one of them, and was irritated that they should remind him – and went about as if he was forever having to get buckets for people.

Ivan walked in with the bridles, knotted together in one hand, and looked at his father and smiled. "Now what are you up to?" he said.

"What am I up to – what do you think – what am I up to – taking care of business, as the song says. You see Margaret?"

"No, I just came – I haven't even been into the house. I promised to give two more riding lessons. I have two really good kids – only ten and eleven – no older than Valerie. I don't know why you won't let Valerie ride –"

"She's not riding and have no horse kick her in the head, let me tell you."

"No horse would kick her in the cocksuckin head – I can get a helmet for her at half price."

"No," Antony said, "she's not fuckin riding – I lost one little child, and I'm not losing another."

And then he went about looking for his bucket.

"Did you go and see Cindi last night?" Antony asked.

"No, I'm not going to either."

"No – either did I," Antony said. "I'm through with all the big hype over that there – I don't care what they do."

Ivan went out of the shed, blinking. The day was windy. Margaret had planted pansies and dahlias along the wall, and he could still see her footmarks where she had stepped about the beds. The impressions were softening to dust, and light sand was blowing up against the west wall of the house.

This reminded Ivan that he had promised to build his grandparents a patio deck this year so they could barbecue and look out at the bay. For some reason he remembered this promise because it was so windy. Now they were barbecuing down by the shed, where Allain used to smoke salmon. He did not smoke salmon any more. Just as, twenty years before, three-quarters of the traffic on the river had to do with work – fishing boats, scows, and pulp boats – now three-quarters of the traffic were people with inboard motor boats and sailboats. It was to this second group that Ruby and her cousin Eugene belonged, while he and Cindi, because of their natures, belonged to the first group, and would always belong to it. Just as Ruby's father, Clay Everette, with over half a million dollars in the bank, would always belong to the first group. And just as Vera and Nevin tried desperately to belong to the first group, they could not by the very way they perceived things belong. At times these groups became blurred and infused, and there was no way to separate them if one did not know what it was to look for. Money had nothing to do with it, nor did age. But still the two groups could be defined. Education might be the key – but that was not true either, although people who wished to make simplistic judgements would use the criteria of money, age, and education to accredit the difference.

As he walked about the west side of the house, he saw Margaret sitting in a lawn chair, reading *Teen* magazine.

"There was a call for you," she said.

Immediately his heart sank when she told him it was not Cindi who had called – but Olive and Gerald Dressard.

"What do they want?"

"I don't know," she said. "Something about coyotes, and you could trap them."

"Well, why didn't you find out?" he said irritably.

He returned the call about thirty minutes later.

"Yes," he said. "I doubt if it's many coyotes – just a mother rounding up her pups."

He found out that Olive was afraid because of her child playing in the yard. Two coyotes had come out to it.

"They're all around us," she said.

"Well, I don't really care to trap them."

Olive said that not only could he have the pelts, but he would be paid also. Then Ivan reflected that it was Adele and Ralphie's child she was talking about.

"I have to boil my traps," Ivan said. "Okay – I'll be over in a few days."

"I don't agree with trapping," Olive said, "but this is a special case."

He went back outside, and, lighting a cigarette, sat on a stump.

"A good man's position is always the right one," Margaret said to him. He stared up at her. She was looking not at him but above his head as she spoke. Then she touched him on the top of the head gently and smiled.

✣   ✣   ✣

There was a general excitement over Vera's pregnancy.

Everything was already done for Vera's baby – everything was already collected – money was already sent and people were already talking about who the baby would look like. Things were largely done that were done everywhere when a pregnancy occurs. And Vera and Nevin were happy that everything was the same.

Now the house that hadn't been a major priority before became one, and it was redone. Because she was pregnant, the whole idea was that she and Nevin knew all along that they would have a child – and that their child was wanted because it was planned for, was a common consensus.

Only Vera seemed to realize that this wasn't quite the way it happened. Of all the doctors they discussed things with, only Dr. Hennessey maintained that she might get pregnant, and the old doctor was the only one they didn't take seriously. Nor did he care if they did.

One night, a couple of weeks earlier, Nevin stayed out until morning. She knew he was now preoccupied with money, and making money. She waited up almost until dawn. When she woke, she was in the spare bedroom and he was sitting looking at her. Nevin had not been home all night – and here he was with his boots, which he prized so much, covered in mud, and his eyes glassy.

"Good morning, Vera," he said tipping a bottle of wine to his lips.

"What do you mean?" Vera said. "Where were you last night –"

"I joined Antony as partners."

"You what?"

"I drank Hermit wine and joined Antony."

Then he reached down and stroked the ears of the rabbit that had followed him down the hallway.

"Well, go to bed," Vera said.

Then he spoke so rapidly that she had trouble following what he said: "We're going to get a big hose and suck every clam alive into it and sell them and make a million dollars."

He looked serious even though she laughed. Then he tipped the bottle to his lips and looked about the room, with its bright new paint, and its crib, as if he'd never seen it before.

"And we will too," he said.

"Well, do what you can," she said, smiling. "Go to bed –"

"Bed," he said. "Of course you don't want to listen to me. You know nothing about it – how could you know." He looked at her sadly while sunlight fell on his boots. "How could you know," he said, cutting an imaginary line with his flat hand through the sunlight, and hiccupping, "if you paid 'tention to me."

"Well – I do," she said.

"No – you don't," he said solemnly, and he rose and wobbled down the hall, stopping now and then because of imaginary barriers.

The night after the party at Ruby's, people began to rock Ivan's cuddy. So he went out onto the wharf. There was no one near the boat except the small dog he had been noticing there since he came. The dog followed him as he walked, looking at him with the inquiring look dogs have when they realize that things have changed in a person's mood.

"There's a big-feelinged lad there," Jeannie said, out of the dark. He couldn't see her, but he knew her voice – utterly plain and yet with a tone unlike any other he had come across – her red hair pinched behind her. Then he did see her gradually standing in the cool air, which, though cool, had a host of mosquitoes hovering in it.

"Ha, ha," Frank said, as he always would answer his wife's insults with a guffaw as if, if no one else in the world recorded them, he himself would. "Odd man out," Frank said.

"How's Cindi?" Jeannie yelled.

Ivan tossed a rock into the water, and looked through the dark, but he couldn't see them any more.

"How's Cindi?" Frank said after. The sound however seemed to come from a different direction altogether.

"Cindi's just fuckin dandy – you dumb cocksucker," Ivan said.

That day another rumour had started – that Cindi had filed for divorce. Ivan, of course, had heard this rumour, the way all characters involved in rumours hear one, as if it were already true and he himself knew about it.

He looked about and then turned back towards the boat. A group of high school kids had come onto the wharf to drink beer and were sitting there watching him. He didn't notice them until this moment. He didn't know them and they didn't know him, but at this moment it seemed as if they did, and that everything that was said was said for their approval.

When he walked by them, he could feel them staring at him. So finally he said, "You hurt this dog?" as if they were the ones to blame.

"I never hurt the dog – is that yer dog?"

Ivan said nothing but took the dog with him to the boat. Then he turned the spotlight on the water, and moved it in the direction of the shale bank.

The only thing that looked back at him was one lone cow standing in mud, with the blank expression an animal has when caught in a beam of light.

"I must be fuckin mad," Ivan said, and he smashed the light with the flat of his hand and sent it sprawling onto the water.

A few moments later, Antony drove along the wharf at ten miles an hour, waving to all the boys Ivan had just accosted, smiling and talking in a loud voice, and stopped just by *The Simonie D.*

"You think he'd name the boat after me," Antony said, "instead of that adopted twit." Simonie was Allain's adopted daughter and was one of the administration nurses in St. John – but whether this was the reason or not, Antony didn't like her, and said she had "stole" his "mom's" affection for the others. Ivan sensed a deep bitterness here, which had struck Antony's heart – and seemed both comic and pathetic.

But still, since Ivan always felt tricked by his father, his one thought was, what in hell does he want now?

The visit was like getting phone calls from people whom you like, but who never consider you until they need something. Antony would never come just for a visit to an old cuddy – he had spent half his life in one, what did he need it for.

Ivan had turned the radio on and had picked up a station in the Gaspé, a French station playing Paul McCartney's "Ram" album – "Monkberry Moon." The music seemed to expand through the little cuddy and across the whole wharf, which smelled of shells and tar and the rind of traps, the wharf being still pale in the night air. Against all parts of the wharf, boats were tied.

Ivan held a bottle of rye in his hand, and Antony noticed it but said nothing.

"Guess who wants to become like me," he said solemnly.

"I don't know," Ivan said.

The radio-band light was orange, but only the bottom side of the dial was lighted. It glowed in the little dark cuddy, and the boat tossed more against the tires.

"Nevin," Antony said, "he asked me the other night if I could make him some money, and I said, 'Sure I can make you some money – how much you need?'"

Antony said this as if everyone knew he could make people a lot of money, and that it was a known fact, and the only naive thing about Nevin was that he had not asked him before.

And as always with new partners, tonight Antony could do nothing but speak about Nevin – as always with Antony, the new partnership had already made all the money, and it was just a matter of picking this money up.

As always with Antony, he was drinking to this new partnership and forgot that he'd been in partnership with Nevin before, and as always if anyone said anything about it, he would dismiss them as not knowing what they were talking about.

"Nevin looks up to me," he said solemnly. "I suppose he and Vera know that whatever I've done I've done on my own."

As the general smell of saltwater, rope, and tar filtered throughout the cuddy, as the radio played, and as there were still lights out in the bay, Ivan was thinking. Every time Antony strayed onto a wharf, he was like a man who one day suddenly grabs the halter of a disgruntled horse and backs it down off the trailer to the amazement of those there. On the wharf there was nothing Antony saw that he did not know, and there was no swell of wave or sound or shade of light that he did not feel or expect. And this was seen in spite of being away from fishing for twenty years. Antony, as a youngster, had fished with his uncle while Allain fished with Antony's older brother.

On the night of the Escuminac disaster, he and his uncle were out in the twenty-eight-foot drifter, *The Margot*.

At first they only thought of riding the storm out, but there were too many other boats in trouble. Ivan had learned that Antony, with a rope attached to him-

122

self, kept every boat in sight as long as he could, but they were continually battered away. The waves, at moments, were seventy or eighty feet high, and their boat was twenty-eight feet long, and their engine, too, seemed to take on a life of its own – unexpectedly heroic.

His uncle, who would be Ivan's great-uncle, was short and broad as he was tall, built as if he had been made out of darkened stone. He had been fishing since he was ten. His nose was huge and crooked, and he had a goiter on his neck, which allowed him to drive his car about without a licence because all the police thought he had cancer and were sorry for him. So he would pile his nine children into the car and drive from Legaceville to Caraquet, everyone sitting on everyone's knees and singing, with the windows rolled down and their legs and arms sticking out, each one of them trying to hold on to their ice cream, roaring and yelling when they saw an out-of-province licence plate, and pausing to take licks.

Once a wave picked him up, held him in the air, as the boat listed beneath him. Then it dropped him down again, and he stood exactly where he had been.

They had tied themselves together, and had attached the rope through two steel hooks along the gunnels. The prow faced the waves and rose up towards them, and then vaulted down again, stern skyward, and hit the bottom of the bay, before it started its determined journey up against the next wave. Antony felt a sharp pain in his left hand when he tried to steer it towards his father's boat. Most of this was forgotten now.

Antony could make out his father's boat behind them, off to the left but only on its rise. He could tell that they had given up trying to make it to the wharf, and were trying now to hold off and ride the storm out. But he knew they would not, and they would have to give it up also, and concentrate on making it to the wharf. Most of this was forgotten.

When they saw the wharf in sight, Antony felt a delight and a sadness overwhelm him because it was not until then did he realize what was happening. Tears flooded his eyes because he saw lights on in the pink-and-white houses, and a pain came to his throat. They had made the wharf safely, and were about to tie.

And then, because they saw the lights in the houses – or because of *The Maralee*, with its wide prow and proud name, which they saw sinking, or of the women waiting in those houses – or *The Denise R.* from P.E.I., so far from her own wharf and struggling to make it to theirs, with her nets tangled behind her and sinking her stern first, they turned *The Margot* about and went back to save whomever it was they could. Most of this was forgotten now.

"Let's go after them," his uncle said, smiling broadly and patting the engine-housing, his smile making his face, covered in sweat and water, crinkle innocently, the same way it did when he piled his nine children into the car, with the little girls wearing dresses, all off to get an ice cream at the corner store.

"Let's go after them," Antony said, his left hand already broken and swollen and burning, so he hid it from his uncle. The boat again chugged out into the waves, leaking oil, to where they'd last seen *The Denise R.* with her bulky nets.

Ivan knew why Antony continually licked his big sapphire ring and took it off and put it on a while

124

later. It was because his left hand ached continually, but he never mentioned why.

Antony, now years later, and thirty pounds heavier, with sad eyes and big red ears, was sweating and pale. His breath was irregular as he puffed on his cigarette. He moved his shoes back and forth and looked out the cuddy window at the night. Every time his breath came up short it was as if he was about to speak. But he did not.

There were lights twinkling out there under the stars, so peaceful, and there were lights on in the houses as well, and the church with its cross lighted up the night sky, and the sounds of honking horns on the main highway, and now and then someone breaking glass, and screeching tires.

"She had a fit," Antony said suddenly, while looking through the window and puffing on his cigarette, the cigarette spark flickering in the dark room, with the smell of oil on an old blanket, where the little dog lay peacefully watching both of them with his eyes open.

"How?"

"I don't know, you'll have to ask Ruby – she knows all about it."

He had been resolved not to mention it. But he was at Nevin's telling him to be up at five in the morning – to start their business. And since Vera and Adele were there, he mentioned it to them.

"She had a fit," he said to Vera. "And," he added, looking quickly at Adele, "I think it's all this trouble-making by certain people that are causing the problem."

The one concern Vera and Nevin had was if this seizure had produced a miscarriage. Although it would probably be best if Cindi had an abortion, they thought that a miscarriage would be a terrible injustice.

Adele refused to speak. She had told Ralphie the day before that she was through with ever speaking about Cindi or Ivan again. If she saw, she said, a bomb coming through the roof, "or one of those Sputniks or something like that there, Ralphie – I'd sooner let us all die for openin my gob about it. I'd just go out and pick blueberries and forget it even happened – 'cause I'm no good to talk to. Everyone says I'm so mixed up and need a *sociology* course." She was dead against sociology now because Ruby was majoring in it – though she did not know exactly what sociology was. But just as Antony was about to change the subject – he wanted to tell them how much Valerie made on her worms – $23.95, and he figured that was pretty fair for worms – Adele spoke up:

"Well, the best thing for her to do is have a goddamn miscarriage – and then none of ya will have any fucking thing more to say about it. There'll be no more tears – just like the little doll, 'No More Tears' – well that's what there will be." Then she sniffed and lit a cigarette and then tiny little puffs of smoke came from her nose.

Antony thought she was making fun of him because of his "No More Tears" doll venture of the Christmas before. (In fact, Adele knew nothing about this.) He had gotten thirty boxes of regular stuffed dolls that "couldn't cry with their nose to an onion," and had passed them off down on the Indian reserve as the

126

authentic "No More Tears." So all the Indian children had the "No More Tears" doll that really had no tears.

He looked at Adele, startled that she knew about this, and Vera said, "DELE," like that.

Nevin looked up.

"I don't fuckin care," Adele said, "let everyone do what everyone does and I'll stay out of it because I'm going to leave this family. I'm going to leave Ralphie – I'm going to leave home. I'm going away – walking fast – maybe then I'll have all this cocksucking racket figured out."

"You must admit," Vera said, smiling naively, "that we have her best in mind."

"Oh, of course," Adele said. "Of course, it's all poor Cindi and such."

"Let's not get all worked up," Vera said.

"Well, then I'm all wrong and stupid, I know," Adele said.

"No one says you're stupid," Vera said.

"Oh, for sure, but things are not always as they always seem!"

Then her eyes flashed, and she looked at Antony, who only stared at her. Then Nevin stood up and walked about the room.

Just as Nevin had never looked angrily at Vera until that moment a few weeks before, when he felt that what was deadly serious was taken lightly, so Adele, who always flew off the handle, went into rages, and kicked her husband – for something to do – now became calm.

"It won't matter, think whatever you will," Adele said. "No one profits from this."

III

10

Cindi's life this summer was like a movie, where all her friends were tantalized by and hoping secretly for more stories to come out of this affair, while telling each other they were not, and hoping it would end. Everyone from Ruby to Vera to Adele was listening and waiting, wondering what was going to happen – as if she were not a person but a character in a movie they were watching. Often, when it ran down a little, they were impatient for something more to happen – and something more had to happen to continue on watching. And every one of them, from Cindi herself to Ruby to Adele, watched this film, from a variety of different places in the theatre, holding on to the idea that they hoped for the heroine, and not knowing that the greatest visual effect was the one in which she was crucified for them.

This idea that she was being crucified, drunk and silly and vacant as she had been in her life, never entered their heads as they were pushing her in that direction. She had been, of course, as far as Vera and certain of the more educated women about, a Christ figure because of her brutal marriage – but in no way because of their own pride and philosophy concerning her.

The more attention had been placed on her, the more Cindi felt part of the collective structure and morality of the gang. Circles revolved about a loosely defined oracle, which she had never belonged to before, and now suddenly belonged to – she had passed that litmus test.

Yet it was a small gang, and shrinking for some want of excitement. But people had come up with the idea that since the Levoy brothers were home they should go and "see to Ivan." And people got excited over this.

The Levoy brothers were distant relatives of Cindi.

They hated Ivan because alone they were no match for him. The second brother was the man Ivan protected Ralphie from at the mines. But these were the people – the Levoy brothers who attacked verbally their old nemesis, and had gained the respect of those who had always more or less been frightened of them.

"The Levoys'll take care of him," Lloyd said, for instance. He said this because he was scared of the Levoys. "Yes, they're the lads for him." And psychologically this seemed to help Lloyd. Praising the Levoys he had become part of the great moral significance of the group.

"Yes – well, the Levoys'll take care of the lad," Ruby said one afternoon. "And, if not, Dorval will – right, Dorval?"

Dorval shrank sheepishly into himself. One time, past summer, when he had too much to drink, he had taken a bolo swing at Ivan, and Ivan caught him so he wouldn't fall. It was because Dorval had always loved Cindi, and had lost her. And that was the worst pain in the world. But Ruby now, and even Cindi, pretended that it had happened much differently, and that Dorval, being as he was from Montreal, could handle a man like Ivan.

"I don't want him hurt," Cindi said, as if she now controlled things.

Now, in the middle of summer, with this happy breed of people who cared for her, she reciprocated the ideas of others as if they were her own.

Most of all at this time she didn't want to be censured by her friends. If she was suddenly important, she didn't want to be not important.

Ivan was gone. She had had a string of men since she was sixteen. She was terrified to tell her mother she was pregnant again – but sooner or later her mother would find out.

"And then we won't be able to help you any more," Ruby said one afternoon.

"Oh," Cindi said, looking up at the sun, as if she'd made an awful mistake. "You won't?"

"I mean, it would make me some kind of Jesus laughing-stock now, wouldn't it – keeping care of Ivan's baby."

(It was Ivan's baby in this case.)

"Oh wow," Cindi said, as if she'd made some pathetic mistake. Cindi used all the same out-of-date expressions she had learned eight to ten years ago and was sometimes surprised that no one else did.

"Don't worry," Ruby said, "I'll take care of everything. I won't let you down."

It was not inherent in Ruby to forgo anything that was new or irreverent – and this is primarily what attracted her to abortion. What umbrellaed her concern was not so much that it would be right, but that it would be rebellious and gain attention. Like every-thing else Ruby did. And Cindi felt those feelings of importance, when she was with Ruby, that she'd only caught brief glimpses of in her life.

She remembered that woman with the short hair on the local TV show saying such kind things about her. No one ever, not even Ivan nor her mother, had talked so kindly about her before.

Perhaps what brought matters to a head was Ernie – that is, the forty-four-year-old friend of Antony's, who had the mannerisms and demeanour of a teenaged boy, and something of the arrogance thereof.

He started to hang about with them, as a member of their group, singing Elvis, and flashing his money about. Every time he came down, Cindi would hide in the bathroom until Ruby got rid of him.

Finally, one night, Ernie approached Cindi as she walked along the road.

"I'll take care of your baby, I will – I'll marry you and take care of it."

It was the only noble gesture Ernie could think of, and he had been thinking of it all summer.

He had been thinking of it since the night he was with Ivan and Antony, and it had blossomed into a full-fledged obsession. He had never made love to a woman. He knew nothing about them, but he had become obsessed by this idea that by being noble he would have a ready-made family – a relationship that just three months before seemed impossible for a man like him, whom people all his life had zeroed in upon and teased.

Something so noble produced a self-righteousness in him as he looked at her, his hair dry and blowing in the wind, his face nicked from a razor, and still weathering the leather jacket in the awful summer heat.

"I don't have my baby," Cindi said.

"What do you mean?" Ernie asked.

"I lost it," Cindi said, "so please don't worry about me any more." And she reached out and touched his face. She held the hand to his face, as if he were a child himself. And then took it quickly away and smiled nervously. Then she turned and walked along the street.

"Here," he said, "you need money" – and he tried to fumble in his pocket – "please," he said, as she walked away, "take it."

Ruby was furious over this intrusion into what was "her concern."

"It's not his problem," she said.

There was a good deal of cynicism from Ruby and Dorval Gene that someone as "ignorant" as Ernie would try to help.

And, finally, a good deal of jovial laughter also.

❖   ❖   ❖

The morning of the appointment, Ruby took Cindi to the site of her new house. They walked across the field, high with goldenrod and dandelions. Far down below they could see the highway and the river as it widened out into the bay.

The air was still and hot, and they followed the fresh road the tractor had made.

"Well," Ruby said, looking sideways at Cindi and then smiling, "how do you like all this?"

Cindi looked at the huge foundation, saw the lumber piled in rows near the road that had just been made, smelled the cement in the sunlight, and sneezed. Then she sneezed again. "It's the biggest place I've ever seen," Cindi said. (She was trying to be polite.)

"Well, it's nice," Ruby said, "but they are *doing* it *wrong* – and I told Big Clay, 'Hey listen, you are doing this wrong,' but I spose what's done is done – hm?" Then she kicked a stone into the foundation as if to prove a point, dusted her hands together, and smiled.

Everywhere they went that morning – from the stable where she brushed her colt, looked at its hooves and immediately took on the look of a person who had been around a stable all of her life, to when she went to pay the bill at Jim's Convenience and played the punchboard, wiggling her bum, to when she went back to the office and told Lloyd that some of the two by eights at the house were split – she became what she was doing, while Cindi followed her. It was as if she didn't know Cindi very well – and wanted to impress her with how competent she was, and all that her own independent life offered her.

And everywhere they went Cindi went after her, smiling when people said things, and nervously waiting for the time to pass.

Then finally it was two o'clock – the time when Dr. Savard would leave the hospital and go to his downriver office.

For some reason, just before the appointment, Ruby was compelled to take Cindi shopping. She took out her credit card and bought her two dresses, a hat for summer, a new bathing suit, some underwear. When Cindi tried on one of the dresses, Ruby said, "There now, that's the new you."

She smiled at Cindi slightly, then frowned, as if this important decision was still painful, and then went over and hugged her. Dresses hung from racks behind them. She felt Cindi's body melt into her, just as Cindi's body melted into anyone she touched, with her tiny eyelashes blinking quickly, and her smile crooked.

Cindi was frightened. She was frightened of the room, and of everything immediately. She was frightened that she would do something, that her body would not look right. Dr. Savard was really a very tiny man, and she stood almost eye to eye with him. So both she and Ruby started to giggle.

He took her blood pressure, and made a joke. Many people said that Savard's accent was soothing – he spoke in a very comforting voice and this reassured many people.

"Now there is no problem here whatsoever," he said. "If you don't want the child, that's quite all right with us – no one here passes judgement upon you."

"I'm ashamed," Cindi said. And she giggled once more. And then held her breath when he looked up.

"Hm." He looked up, as if he was puzzled. "Hm – oh – don't be." But one could tell he hadn't understood why she said this.

He asked her how she was feeling, and busied himself asking questions that she tried to answer quickly.

She did not want to be frightened of things. And because they were *supposed* to like each other, they pretended to themselves that they did. But Savard in other circumstances would have had nothing to do with her. And Cindi knew this. So she had nothing to say.

This fear Cindi had of everything around her persisted throughout the questioning. She just wanted to get it all over and go home. She disliked Dr. Savard when she thought she would like him. And she mistrusted his soothing voice.

Cindi, when she looked at him, sneezed, and then sneezed once more – and then again. "Dust," she said. He smiled. She reminded him, in fact, of one of Fortune's daughters who was always doing poorly in school. Outside his office there was a gravel lot that ran far away to an old road, with a cul-de-sac sign, the post of which had been painted green, and a long darning needle flew out of the bushes and in front of the sign, moving here and there in the afternoon light.

Then there were some trees also, little ones, their branches looking sticky and hot, and there was a feeling of humidity. The sun hit the front grill of his Porsche, which was parked near the window – he had parked the car at the back because near the front entrance the children would put their fingers on it.

Since Cindi was nearing the end of the first trimester, he might have sent her to Moncton – but because of what happened today, he pretended to himself not to think of it.

Earlier in the day, Savard had made a decision concerning a pregnancy. And he was convinced it was the right decision. A woman had so much fluid at seven months that her kidneys had shut down. Savard took her husband aside and said: "We *can* save the child but we *can't* save her."

The husband had just come from work. He had gotten a call that his wife had been taken to the hospital.

"Well, she won't stay here," the young man said, almost immediately. "She's been to you before and nothing was wrong. And now yer tellin me – telling us – about it and everything," he said, losing control, and looking about. "She won't stay here – she'll go down to Moncton." And at the word Moncton, he broke down and started to cry, saying, "She'll go to Moncton – she will – we'll go to Moncton." Savard did not know what to do.

He spoke in French to one of the nurses, who immediately began to rub the young man's back tenderly. Savard did not think the woman would last an hour, and he wanted to save the child.

Just at that moment Dr. Hennessey walked out of the small supply room behind them. And Savard could not help but feel that the old doctor had been listening to everything and made his appearance just at this time as if on cue. "Well," he said, looking down at the boy, "why do you want to go to Moncton? What in hell is there in Moncton – what's wrong?"

Savard gave him the details about Brenda.

"Nonsense," Hennessey said, "that's little Brenda Corrigan – nonsense altogether."

And when Hennessey said this, Savard felt he was being criticized because Hennessey did not like him. He felt Hennessey looked upon him as an enemy, who was "open" to "change." There was something appealing in Hennessey – in his ability to remain unopened to change. Savard could recount a dozen times that Hennessey went contrary to opinion just because of pride.

"She went into shock in the case room," he said softly, as if Hennessey would be won over by this.

"Well," Hennessey said, "if *you* can't help her, get an ambulance ready. Get – who will we fetch – Rose

Wong – get Rosy Wong with her and we'll send her down."

And with that, Hennessey started to give orders to two nurses at the station across the hall, who were pretending to be busy with forms but who had been listening to everything.

Within ten minutes there was an ambulance, the R.N., Rose Wong, a driver, and Dr. Hennessey – and though Savard helped with all of this, prepared the woman who was twenty-two years old, he felt that it was a useless token, and that she wouldn't be able to make the trip.

Just before Cindi had arrived, he had found out that the woman was now doing fine. And for some reason, people are irritated when they are wrong. "I'm glad," he said. But secretly he was not.

Ruby felt she had to let Savard know that she also was here and so she continually touched, patted, and kissed Cindi. And Cindi kept saying, "Phew – don't smother me Rube – go way."

But suddenly when the procedure started Ruby started to laugh out loud and Savard looked over at her with the perplexed look of a young boy. Then she felt embarrassed by this and left the room. She shook, and felt cold and frightened. The idea of attracting attention to herself was gone. She sat in the waiting room. Suddenly, from behind the door, she could hear Cindi sigh, as if she was being hurt. Cindi sighed, and said, "Oh, oh." Ruby put her hands over her mouth, and then she went for a walk.

She walked along the road to the Dairy Bar and bought herself an ice cream, and sat out on a bench in the yard. She waved now and then to some people who drove by whom she knew, and felt a strange sudden glee, which she tried to deny that she felt.

Cindi wanted to go home almost immediately. She kept looking out the window because she couldn't look at Dr. Savard. No more anger had ever come over her than at this moment. She was angry with everyone, especially Ivan and herself.

"How do you feel?" he said finally. He was wearing a short-sleeved summer shirt. This, plus his tan, seemed to make a tremendous impact on her. He was reading a magazine at his desk. The first time he had asked her that question it sounded to Cindi very different. That was because the emphasis on the word "feel" was different – it had a very different meaning. This time, in spite of, or because of, Savard's gentle way of asking it, it did not mean, how do you feel physically, but how do you feel in some other deeper more poignant way. And Cindi nodded, averted her eyes, and tapped her foot as if impatient with something. "Sure," she said suddenly, "I'm fine."

Ruby returned with ice cream for them.

Savard didn't seem to know what to do with his ice cream. He squinted as he held it, with a napkin about the cone, but didn't take a lick. Nor did Cindi want hers, until Savard said it might be good if she ate it. They spoke, all of them, about the variety of ice cream flavours now available, and teased Cindi when she said she liked vanilla. All the talk was appropriately low-key.

Then Savard locked the office and they went outside. The day had turned windy, and small typhoons blew about the parking lot, scattering dust and sand.

They all stood together talking, and Savard smiled

at Cindi. But she felt the smile a half-hour before was much different.

The sun was falling on the trees in back of them and Cindi was shivering, her ice cream melting on her dress.

Ruby was excited, but when Cindi looked at her and smiled clumsily, she didn't look back. Then for some reason she started to curse and swear over nothing at all, turning for some reason violently angry that her car wasn't clean.

✛ ✛ ✛

Armand Savard was the thirteenth child of nineteen children, and the only one who saw high school or university.

His father worked himself to death, and looked like a ghost at forty, and they ate porcupine all one summer and gave their money to the Catholic church. This is what Armand remembered about his youth.

He trembled whenever he told this story. All his brothers and sisters in the tar-paper shack in summer, while Mr. Bellia stood at the door in his suit, and asked his father to take some friends of his from Sherbrooke fishing out in the bay.

He saw his father smiling without a tooth in his head, and his mother pregnant and sitting on a chair in the corner, while the whole dusty little kitchen smelled of flies and rancid butter. And contrasted to this, the bay looked so blue and clean outside their door.

Sometimes, walking home in the summer, there would be beautiful smells of food coming from the house. His mother would be baking bread for the Feast of the Assumption.

Savard hated these memories, and he was ashamed of his family. He never drove his Porsche there, and he never took his wife there. He was also frightened of his older brother, Fortune, who was a drunk. But it was Fortune who knew that Armand was ashamed of them, and he couldn't look Fortune in the face.

Fortune, one time, brought him over ten bottles of pickled herring that his wife had done, and then he found them in the dump the next week. Fortune never spoke of it, and when Armand spoke about how good the pickled herring was, he looked over Armand's right shoulder into the distance.

Fortune had paid for Armand's education. Armand, on the surface, became a meticulous and sophisticated teenager – the kind that only an Acadian can be, with a worldly outlook even though he lived in a shack – while his sisters got married at sixteen and seventeen and his brothers worked in the woods.

He married a woman from Sackville, and he had always felt superior to her, and, as people noticed, superior to women in general. They had four children.

Fortune was a huge, ignorant man, who had hardly learned how to read and write, who was frightened to go into restaurants, and yet Armand had secretly always looked up to him and tried to impress him.

Armand remembered a group of English kids one day had surrounded him at the beach, and how Fortune had come over and had willingly taken the beating to protect his younger brother. And though he was ignorant and went to church just like his father and mother, and blessed himself every time he passed the big church down river, and had his wife bake for the Feast of the Assumption – just like his mother – Armand always felt that he had to prove himself to this man, who so willingly had taken a beating for him when they were youngsters, and had paid for his first suit in 1966.

No matter what Armand did, he could not impress him and the fault lay in the fact that he tried to impress him, with talk that Fortune did not care about or understand. Fortune would only shrug, and even pick at his nose with the flat of his finger and stare morosely about, as if wanting to be impressed left him disappointed.

Fortune didn't understand things about his brother. He didn't understand about the pills he gave out – Fortune never had a pill in his life – or the operations. But he still thought the world of his brother.

One day he was told that his brother performed abortions, and all the young women would go to him and have them.

It was a spiteful old woman who had no children of her own, who had always hated their family, who told him, but Fortune was upset. He went home and asked his wife about it. First he had to know what an abortion was. His wife told him.

For Fortune, this was the worst thing in the world. He didn't understand it. He couldn't understand it, and the more he tried, the more it worried him. He did not want to tell his mother. His father had died years ago – a horse had kicked him in the back.

"No, I won't tell Mama," he said, and this seemed to relieve him.

There was still sun on the ground and he went out for a walk.

He walked by Armand's office – which before had seemed so important to him. But now, to him at least, it only seemed lonely and entirely insignificant, with sunlight on the window – as if it had been always meant to be there, but Armand himself did not know this.

"It's better," Armand told him, when he asked about it. Fortune was so shaken up he could hardly ask. He didn't understand it. But Armand really didn't know how to explain it and only could say: "It's better."

"It's better," Fortune nodded in a peculiar way. He thought his brother would deny it. But Armand, looking up at him over the top of a magazine, only said: "It's better."

He told him that there were lots of young girls now who got pregnant, and had no other recourse – some were raped or molested, or unmarried. But at any rate they did not want to bring unwanted children into the world, and anyway, it was better – he had always agreed with it. Besides, he only did fifteen or twenty a year.

"Fifteen or twenty," Fortune said, his broad ignorant back, in a woollen shirt catching the sun. Armand looked at his brother. Fortune's eyes showed that he was in disbelief. He sat there, with his hands folded together. Two of his big brown fingers were missing. He had lost them with an axe, when Armand was fifteen.

"Fifteen or twenty."

"Oh, you'll understand," Armand said, smiling and trying to be reasonable. "Of all people you should know how Mom suffered with all of her children. It's a good thing if they are unwanted and an unneeded burden."

Armand had been premature. When he was born they put him in a shoe box near the stove. He was so tiny. Even now his eyes were weak, which made him appear more meticulous than he actually was, and he had allergies and caught colds. Fortune was always asking about his health, and every Christmas Fortune's wife knitted Armand a sweater.

"And that's the problem – they are unwanted," Armand was saying. "And will end up as a burden, in jail or something, and you take how many kids are abused – or things like that."

Fortune sat with his head down, as if he was being scolded. The big shoulders were still, and Armand could not help remembering how men had jumped on those shoulders when Fortune was protecting him, while he himself was frightened, and only managed to run away.

And Armand looked at those strong burdened shoulders, and felt sad when he remembered how the men had hit his brother with a stone over the head.

Strange how men see things. Mrs. Savard, who had a pale-reddish complexion, and deep lines under her eyes, whose hair was too long, and hung down her back when she pushed her shopping cart with her four children, took pills.

And that's why Fortune thought their lives were so above his own, and why he thought Jennifer Savard was so beautiful.

If she was not frail, if she did not laugh at the wrong time because she was nervous, if she did not get tired, Fortune would not have thought this. And each of her kids had a problem of some slightly indefinite nature. One was hyperactive and had painted his entire body silver and walked to school. The oldest girl, who was twelve, still sucked her thumb.

There was also a problem with their education. To Fortune, they always seemed to be bussed somewhere. They just did not go to school like everyone else – which Fortune's wife mistook as being very grandiose. But because there was a fight between Mr. and Mrs. Savard about where they should go to school, the children were sent one place and then another with no real foundation. The youngest, a boy who looked so much like Armand, went to a French kindergarten.

Armand and Jennifer lived in a huge brick house near the edge of the village – two miles down the road from where Armand had grown up, and, in fact, quite near the local dump. His wife hated it there. It smelled of burnt embers in the dying autumn sunlight, smelled of the ghosts of fishing nets, and the pale empty sky.

But Armand could think of nowhere else to go.

One day last autumn the oldest girl, Teddy, had pooped herself at a recital at school. Armand and Jennifer had not known there was a problem. But now they did all the things other middle-class families did. They got her to a psychiatrist, in Moncton, three times a month.

Jennifer was the one who took her, and paid for it. She drove the long monotonous tortured way, through Rogersville – in the spring it didn't seem to be a road at all but just a grey ugly marker.

Jennifer had her own bank account. Armand never gave her any money and they were in debt, but still and all she managed to save fifteen hundred dollars – and this was the money she used for Teddy.

Teddy sucked her thumb and stared out the window as they drove back and forth.

What the psychiatrist doubtlessly found out was what Fortune had seen. Their large house was empty. There were one or two pictures on the walls, but Armand didn't collect art like people thought. He'd only seen two pictures that he'd liked, and thought that he should collect them. Other than that the house was large and barren, and certain parts of it seemed to crack. The worst of it was it was entirely new. The psychiatrist likely found out from Teddy that Jennifer hated it, especially in November before the snow – when the ground, and the windows were raw, and the whole sky seemed to bleed into the earth.

And the psychiatrist might have found out about the bicycle. All last summer Daniel, the boy who'd painted himself silver, wanted a bicycle. But they just couldn't go to a store.

Armand was against that. It was here where his meticulous nature showed itself. It was always shown in a slightly perverse way, over seemingly mundane things.

"No, I'm not going to a store here," he said.

And when they asked why, he said that he didn't want others, especially in his family, to know their business.

And so they ordered a bike from the catalogue. And there began the wait. Daniel waited the whole summer for his bicycle to come on the bus.

He would go down to the small store where the bus pulled in every afternoon, and wait on the steps with his two sisters. But the bike did not come. Until August. And when it did come, it was not like other bikes.

It wasn't like the bikes in the store window. It hadn't been put together.

Jennifer was so outraged at this final wound to her child she refused to allow Fortune to put it together. The children had naturally run to Fortune, who had taken them fishing, who had helped them make kites.

But when he came over to put the bike together, Jennifer said, "No, his father will."

And the boy stood in the breezeway crying. Fortune nodded simple-heartedly. He smelled of holy water, which his wife gave him to bless the bike.

Finally, in September, Jennifer and Teddy got the instructions out. The air was filled with the smell of heavy rain and already the leaves were blowing from the trees through the banging breezeway doors.

Then the youngster got on the bike, went round the lane as fast as he could, shifted gears, looked back, and waved to his mother, who stood alone at the side of the garage, watching him. Then the handle bars came loose, and the wheel wobbled, and they had to put it away.

Perhaps the psychiatrist learned that Jennifer thought Armand shouldn't leave them alone so much, which showed in the summer when he spent time with his friends at the lodge far away from them in Doaktown and played golf fanatically, while they sat in a rented cottage in Shediac. Perhaps this is what the fights were about – about the veneer of life that Armand had rested his hopes on – which he took to be worldly.

Perhaps the psychiatrist had no answers for them. But after a while, they stopped going to her.

Now, Jennifer was sometimes seen driving her old Datsun station wagon through town, chain-smoking, with one or two of the kids in the back seat.

Because of the emptiness in their lives, the seeming emptiness, at any rate, Jennifer started to take the children to Mass. She looked helpless with her four children in church.

Not a Catholic herself, she did not know when to genuflect or bless herself – and two of the children had not been to church before.

Jennifer had lost her direction, and only wanted to do something for her children whom she loved.

The priest, Father LeBlanc, the same priest who had hit Ivan, had now reformed himself. It was a hard struggle – but that's what life is finally about – and he had become a kinder, gentler man. He had not lost his temper in twelve years.

Perhaps at first he wasn't meant to be a priest, as many priests perhaps aren't. But over the years he realized that he had a God. He always had been an abrupt, short-tempered Frenchman, with dark blistering eyes. But he had seen the wounded, the ill, and the sick, and he found out he could help them by counting himself among them.

And there was prosperity also – he knew some ten millionaires who had made their money on what fascinated Antony so much, the snow-crab industry. But with their money came more problems, rivalry amongst the family members that was unheard of before. And he walked amongst them, carrying the stigma of his past, his bullying, his bigotry, like a rock up a hill.

He often thought about Ivan, whose name he did not remember, and whose whereabouts he did not know. But that was one of the regrets of life, the inability to atone to those sad contemplative faces, which visit you in the dark or when the snow is falling down.

Jennifer and her children helped him as much as he helped them. Because he laughed good-naturedly with them – all the children wanting to go to confession immediately because they had terrible sins to confess.

They seemed to cling to him, too, as if they were insecure birds.

But when Jennifer was making plans for Teddy's confirmation she began to lose sight of what she wanted. After a while they didn't come back. Where they stood, all about him near the altar that day, all ready to confess to great crimes, with Jennifer smiling on their behalf, seemed now to be an empty spot.

He didn't see the children again unless they were driving with their mother in the old Datsun station wagon, the brake lights caked with mud.

He discovered that it was Jennifer herself. She had turned, bolted in another direction, looking for another way.

Savard spent a good deal of time with Ruby. And for a while that summer he believed the reason he was free was because he was trapped. If he wasn't trapped by his marriage, then he couldn't possibly show how he was broad-minded enough to be free.

Savard felt estranged now from his own children. They all looked at him with wounded eyes, they all seemed to think he was a contributor to their unhappiness.

It was not just the bicycle. It was the light fixtures for the house. He had to argue with salesmen so much, and be so abrupt, that finally he didn't buy any. And so the light fixtures did not come, and bare bulbs hung from the walls and ceilings.

151

Everyone talked about his car, but he hid it, and sometimes he would not park it in his yard, but in the garage down the street.

When Savard swung a golf club, one could see how impatient he was by his short, fierce little chops. And he would always look about after he swung the club, as if he had demonstrated something in his nature that he secretly disliked and was trying to improve.

He did not give his wife money. And at the grocery store they would stand together, and in front of people he would count out the tens and twenties she would have to use to pay for the food, with a golf tartan on his head, his hair curly. He was shorter than his wife by three inches.

Other men had done this, he had seen it all his life, and he would do it also.

His oldest boy was forty pounds overweight and took piano lessons at the Ecole Musique from Mrs. McGraw. And when Jennifer drove her children downtown, his huge head was seen in the back seat, in the middle of his siblings' little heads.

Armand couldn't give up his family – that is, his own brothers and sisters. Almost to a man, or woman, they envied him, so there were no light fixtures in his house, and there was no bicycle from a store, and there was no new car for his wife – and his wonderful car, which he couldn't afford, sat in a garage down the street.

Except for Fortune, his brothers sneered at him, phoned him drunk in the middle of the night to bawl him out for giving them the wrong medicine, and then seeing him the next day they would be overcome with shame, apologize, and ask for money.

He hated it here and yet he wouldn't go.

This idea that Ruby and he cared for each other came partly from this.

But gradually he found that she wanted to be seen and needed to do things that attracted attention to herself. One day she followed him about the golf course, laughing whenever he hit a shot poorly. She was wearing a short summer skirt and a loose top, so the nipples of her breasts were visible.

And, later that afternoon, when they were alone, he had to make up a lie and tell her that he was happy she had come. And she simply looked at him, and snapped a match to light her cigarette.

Armand liked to believe he didn't consider these things wrong – the church he hated did. Yet once he found himself embroiled with Ruby, he was priggish, deep in his heart. This priggishness was borne out in tantrums at home and in his needless anger with Jennifer and the children.

His oldest son's birthday was the day Cindi went to the office. Coming into the house he gave his wife and children a terrible lecture. That was brought on because of the nervousness he felt over the abortion. Why did they wait for him? Didn't they know – what? Wasn't he busy?

They had not wanted to cut the cake until their father got home, and yet he was angry and didn't want any cake. Jennifer tried to be happy, but this only dampened his mood, and he callously derided his son for being overweight. Then he went to leave the dining room.

Only then Armand realized that his son's friend – a little girl from the Ecole Musique – was standing behind him. Up until this point she had been smiling. But, when Armand noticed her, she looked frightened.

Suddenly she turned and tried to run away.

Before Jennifer got to her, she was at the back door. Armand could hear her trying not to cry.

He turned to go to the little girl to apologize.

Then he looked at his son.

"You shouldn't have more than two pieces," he said, trying to be brave and joke.

He felt ashamed. He went upstairs, and phoned the Moncton Hospital to see how Brenda Corrigan was doing. And at this moment he was deeply concerned and wished he could have acted better towards her. He remembered how Brenda spoke, with such a twang, and suddenly he loved the memory of her voice because it reminded him of all things that were innocent.

"Tell her husband to phone me," he said.

He put the phone it its cradle and sat all night in the dark.

After Ruby brought Cindi to his office – a small, slow girl with a damp face – whom he for some reason (he did not know why) did not like and could not look in the eye – the summer was finished for them both.

He wanted to act kindly to his family but he did not know how. Jennifer painted the kitchen cupboards. She was obsessively painting. The air was scalded with paint, which Armand was allergic to, so it was like a bright yellow hell.

And Ruby flew zigzagging into the dark once again.

11

Though both Eugene and Cindi were scared of Ruby, both of them pretended to themselves and to each other that they weren't. He did not know why he felt he musn't disappoint Ruby, but he knew he was certain of doing it sooner or later.

The very idea that he was from Montreal allowed Ruby to control everything by saying: "Well you understand – you're from Montreal."

And so he would walk about understanding things, being from Montreal.

In fact, all about him was proof that things were just as accessible here as they were anywhere else. And within everything, within the parties, the lobster boils, and the convertible rides at night, within all of this, from the Mateus wine he got sick on to his spontaneous acceptance that he was from Montreal and therefore was cosmopolitan enough to agree with things – within all of this was a falseness about his position that he understood, and he knew that everyone else did too.

He was also, as many men are of women they know, frightened of Ruby's temper. When she got angry he witnessed some terrible scenes, in the house and at work. She had taken her last car, a Pinto, and had driven it through a tavern window because her high school boyfriend was sitting with someone she didn't like. And when she got angry, as all people, she was compelled to continue and delighted in her ability to lose control.

By now the hot flagging days, the retarred roadways, the dust-covered leaves, the shapes and smells of flat tires hanging down from silent backyard branches, made everyone in the group tired of one another. Dorval wanted to go home, back to Montreal.

"You have to stay with me and help me out," Ruby said. "Besides, what's in Montreal?"

Cindi would stand between them, looking up at one, and then at the other, as they argued.

"What's in Montreal?" Dorval would say. But then he would shrug, look out the open window with its chipped paint ledge, and stare down at a few dusty small sparrows twittering near a puddle in the dirt parking lot.

"You don't have to stay on my account," Cindi would say. "I'm fine."

Her mother had come down finally to visit her, and kept hoping that Cindi wasn't causing all kinds of trouble for them. Cindi sat rigidly at the other end of the metal table and watched everyone with eyes of terror. Her mother was still trying to look like an actress out of the fifties. She was good-natured and only wanted to be part of the good time everyone seemed to be having here. Now and then she put her hand on Dorval's thigh, and patted it maternally.

"I had a baby, Mom – but I lost it," Cindi said.

"Yes," her mother said, lighting a cigarette and dropping the lighter back into her purse. "Well, I've heard that – haven't I." And when she raised her eyes to stare at Cindi, Cindi looked about the table as if searching for a kindly face, and then sat with her head down. Now and then she moved one of her fingers along the tabletop. When she looked up, her mother was just turning to look towards her again, and her head dropped as if she had a weight on it and her eyes closed, with her bottom lip turned out.

Ruby wanted a larger group but Cindi did not want to go anywhere. She was tired of meeting people and just wanted to stay by herself.

Ruby bought her ice cream, talked of taking her to the shrine at Sainte-Anne-de-Beaupré because Cindi wanted to go there, but the morning they got ready to go, Cindi said she didn't feel like it.

Dorval then bought Cindi a puppy.

It had brown ears and a white tail.

Every once in a while Cindi would put her hand out and the puppy would lick it.

But then one morning she said that they should take the puppy back.

So they packed the puppy, and its flea collar, leash and rubber bone, in the box it came in and took it back to the pet shop in the mall. All it did was wag its tail against the box when it saw Cindi, and try to nuzzle her dress with its nose. Sometimes when they walked through a mall, Cindi would drop back twenty or thirty paces, and stare down at the floor. Ruby would have to go back to get her. And Cindi, wearing a pantsuit the colour of a lima bean, would, in the illogical stubborn way slow people have to protect themselves, start to argue with her.

"No, you don't have to come back."

"No – I'm all right."

"No – I don't have a problem, Ruby – you are making a scene."

Ruby would have to make sure Cindi took her phenobarbital – but she herself kept forgetting to give it to her, and then would wake her up in the middle of the night to take it.

Ruby did not understand why, but there were always terrible arguments after they went to bed.

"Well, I don't like you today, Cindi."

"No – you never liked me, Ruby. You always said things about me."

"No – I never did – you are all mixed up and gone bonkers again. I never disliked you, but I do today, young lady."

"You called me retarded – so howdya like that?"

"My God, woman, I never did in my life."

"And told Dr. Savard I was slow – like I didn't graduate or something like that."

"I never said a thing. Who told you that –"

"I could tell by his questions."

Ruby would say nothing.

"No one could think I could tell by their questions. . . ."

(Pause.)

"No one could think I could tell – I could tell by their questions. . . ."

(Pause.)

"And I didn't like Dr. Savard either."

"Well that's not up to me, is it?"

"You thought I'd like him."

"I didn't say that –"

(Pause.)

"Ha."

"No, I didn't – it was always up to you, so don't point the finger of blame."

(Long pause.)

"And I'm not in love with Dorval Gene and you think I am."

"I never said you were," Ruby would say.

"You told Dorval Gene I was –"

"I never said anything so ridiculous –"

"Ask Dorval – he thought I was – he bought me a pin for my blouse."

"Well la-tee-da to that."

(Pause.)

"That's what you think."

"Cindi, go to sleep it's late, dear."

"And you think everyone's not as smart as you."

"There's lots of people a lot smarter than me," Ruby would say in the late-at-night resigned tone brilliant people have about the limitations of their own brilliance.

"Ha."

Ruby would be lying in her sleeping bag on the far side of the living room, Cindi in her blanket and cushion on the other side. The shadow of the wharf light would just reach them through the long window. The maple would wave in the dark. There would be a long pause.

"You only like Dr. Savard because he reminded you of Missle Ryan."

Ruby wouldn't say anything. She would open her eyes and look at the wall.

"And I'm going to Sainte-Anne-de-Beaupré – I'm going by myself."

She paused. "Some time soon."

Ivan had taken the day to scout where the coyotes were behind the fields. Then, having decided where he would place his traps, he walked through the woods – this was just at dark – and came out on a dirt road. The air smelled of heavy leaves and sandpiles on the side of the road. Limp telephone lines hung in the dusk on lime-coated poles, and the air seemed to tick and fill with pleasant sounds.

He had to walk back to the car, found it when it was pitch black, and went back to the wharf. The evening then turned cold and a rain started falling. The waves beat against the boat and the old tires scraped the side of the wharf. There was a smell of wood and tar in the rain, and the bay was fogged in. Ivan went into his cuddy and saw his father sitting on the cot.

"Cindi lost her baby," Antony said looking at him.

"How?"

"I don't know," Antony said, blowing his nose. "It beats me."

"Well, what happened – where is she?"

"Oh, she's at the apartment there – big-feelinged Ruby won't let me see her."

There was a pause, and Antony looked up at him.

"Some people say you beat her so bad she lost her child."

"Who said?"

"Oh, all that Jesus crew. They were here an hour ago to get you – Frank and Jeannie Russell – with her cousins – the Levoys."

Ivan sat on the old bait box. He was wearing a jean jacket that his arms looked very tight in, a big buckle on his belt, and work boots that were still covered with blades of grass and one small daisy from walking in the woods.

Antony neglected to tell Ivan that he had come onto the wharf with everyone else – saying the same things everyone else did, and feeling that he, too, could generate the same amount of self-important disdain as everyone else. In fact, Antony, in spite of his good intention, had pretended to Frank Russell that he had just heard of this mix-up and wanted to get to the bottom of it. He kept touching Jeannie's little shoulder and shaking his head. The small dog Ivan had adopted had tried to keep them off the boat by running along the gunnels and barking, driving its paw into a nail. Cindi's cousins, the Levoys, were furious because they had just heard that Ivan had beaten Cindi – they had just come home for the summer, and this fact alone made them feel justified.

Ivan knew he was in a terrible position. He couldn't rely on anyone at the moment – and his perception had always served him well. He knew very well that, no matter his own part, he had become a scapegoat in some larger affair that he had no control over, until it ran its course. Frank or Jeannie Russell or his father had no control over it either. And he looked at his little dog – with the brown ears, sitting on its mat, licking its cut paw – proudly believing that his barking and running along the gunnels had kept the men away, when the men had gone away simply because they believed they could find him somewhere else.

In the cuddy light, in the damp, with his hair wet and hanging across his forehead, Ivan looked like

Cindi. Instead of feeling ashamed – as Antony was expecting (and somehow hoping) – Ivan looked tremendously proud and defiant.

"She lost her child," he said, after a long time. "Well, then she'll have another one with someone someday."

Ivan tried to think back to the night of the community centre dance. It was true he had gone there with his buck knife on – but that was because he had been in the woods for most of the day. And he hadn't used it anyway. But now there were those who said he went there with the clear intention of using it. Some would say it because they had heard others say it, others would repeat it.

"One person you've got to admire though," Antony said, looking at him and huffing and puffing as if he was out of breath, "is that Dr. Savard. You know he was brought up in a tar-paper shack – and now tonight I saw him going along in his Porsche –"

"I've seen it," Ivan said.

Antony shook his head, as if to show by physical movement the admiration his words couldn't.

"Of course he pulled over when he saw me, the big wave and 'How are you, Antony.' I used to take Gloria down to him – not like Clay Everette. I was over there last month and Gloria was on the porch lying on the couch, so I went out to the office and saw Clay. I told him, 'You get that little girl to a doctor before she dies,' and Clay looked at me and hung his head. I threw my arms up in the air and said, 'I'm some sick of the whole lot of ya. You've got a spoiled rotten girl in Ruby – who the first year at university had affairs with this married professor – a half a dozen affairs with this married guy – and then because she gets her snit up, you build her a house or something like that. But I don't want her around my Margaret,' I said to them. Clay said, 'Ya, and when was she ever with Margaret?' And I just said, 'That jeesless Dorval Gene and her are going around with all the young pussy on the road – and Margaret is too young to be with the likes of them – and if I see her with them any more, I'll come right over here.'

"After that Clay says to me, 'Look, do you want yer old job back,' and I give him a look. 'No,' I said, 'you keep yer job, and every job like it.'

"'But we want you back,' Clay said. 'Yer the only man who can handle a grader.'"

The truth was, Antony was a magnificent tractor and grader operator.

"Yes," Antony said. "Asked me in front of Lloyd to come back and take over – and I went over to Lloyd and touched him on the shoulder – he was hanging his head too. 'Look,' I said, 'the job's yours as long as you want it, because I won't come back to work here.'

"'But how will you live?' Lloyd said, and I said, 'I'll live because I don't bow to no one and stay true to myself.' And with that I turned and walked back to my truck with Gloria watching out the window at me. Then she comes to the door and runs down in her housecoat. 'Tony,' she says, 'Tony,' and, hanging on to my arm, she tries to drag me back for a big reconciliation with Clay. 'Ya've gotta talk to big Clay,' she says. 'He's offerin you a job –'

"'Don't take it,' Valerie yells out to me – she was sitting in the truck. 'Don't take it, Daddy – please don't take it.' And with that Gloria looks at Valerie and starts to cry." Antony finished up, and he, too, had tears in his eyes.

Just as a story had been fashioned that the woman they took to Moncton had almost died because Dr. Hennessey was her doctor, so, too, did certain people believe that Ivan had beaten Cindi and she had lost her child. And though Antony spread this rumour all over the river, whenever Ivan was in at the house to see Margaret, Antony would convince himself he had only Ivan's interest at heart.

✧ ✧ ✧

By the third week of July, Cindi was no longer at the apartment with Ruby. She had come back home and wouldn't go outside. Dr. Hennessey went over one day to see her.

She looked terrible. Her face was bumpy – just as Ruby said.

He asked her how she was, and then, without being asked, he gave her a quick check over, satisfied himself that she was still on her medication, berated her for not eating.

"Well, you don't look too bad, but," he said quickly, "you've had at least one seizure since I've seen you – and probably two –"

"I had three," Cindi said. "I'm near up to five a month now – that was how bad I was in high school."

"Three, yes, well three – and what's this Ivan business about – why don't you see him?"

"He won't come to visit me," Cindi said.

"Well – I'm sure he isn't the best husband in the world, the little bastard, but I don't believe he tried to knife you either. And when you look back on it, it was very exciting for some people – very gratifying to pretend he had that in mind."

"I don't know," Cindi said. "I was there and he did walk in with his knife."

"Well, think what you want," the doctor said irritably, and then he realized he had frightened her – and that she had spent half of her life frightened of people and he felt angry with himself because of this. "But I don't think he wanted to knife you – and if I had to trust someone – well, he would be a person I would trust – MORE THAN A LOT OF THEM!" he finished up, screeching.

The red building was hot, and the curtains hung limp above the sink. When the doctor came in, Cindi was sitting near the bedroom door, as if hiding behind a cardboard box. She told him the only one to visit her since she'd come back was Margaret. Margaret came to visit her in the daytime.

"Oh yes, and what about that Ruby?" Dr. Hennessey said. "Not that she's any of my business – it's just that you were as thick as porcupine quills in a dog's arse a week ago – something happen?" he asked innocently, with his face looking suddenly almost like a little boy's, and, in spite of himself, beaming in delight.

"Ruby's mad at me," Cindi said, rubbing one thumb against the other and looking at her feet. Then she looked at him. "I bug her," she said, drawing a deep breath and exhaling, as if the fact that she "bugged her" was insurmountable, and not to be questioned.

"And what about that Adele – where the hell is she anyways? She was a friend of yers, wasn't she?" Dr. Hennessey said loudly.

The whole idea that Cindi needed someone to stay with her was paramount not only to the doctor but to Cindi herself – who had become so depressed that she hadn't washed in a week, and yet kept putting on new makeup every day, so that the doctor thought she looked like a cake.

"Ha," the doctor said, "maybe we should get Dr. Savard to come here and sit with you –"

Then, realizing he'd overstepped his bounds, he became silent for a moment.

"Everything is happening on this river today," he said.

With that he shook his head, and, digging into his pocket, took out eighty dollars and laid it on the telephone table beside her.

Cindi was too nervous of him to say anything about this – although in every gesture and movement he showed that he wished to be loving and kind.

"There's lots of ways people hide bigotry from themselves," the doctor mumbled. "Today's way is progressive concern."

Four days later Adele moved down with Cindi on Hennessey's request. The first thing was to get a fan for the apartment, and she took Cindi up to the mall and bought one.

"Now we'll have some cool air at night," she said.

Cindi looked at her and smiled.

"Now, dear," Adele said, "the first thing you got to do is take a bath –"

"I don't want to," Cindi said.

"I don't care if you want to – you're going to," Adele said. "You fuckin stink – and you have more powder than face."

Her only concern was getting Cindi to take some action and make her do something.

"And burn them fuckin clothes," Adele said. "You've been sleeping in them for a week or more, it looks like – and what's this all over the floor here? I don't know – this place is a Christless mess, Cin – you know bettern that."

Cindi was as depressed as she was at times before she had a seizure, something which she almost never recognized in herself but which Adele recognized instantly.

12

Antony had acquired thirty-seven velvet portraits of Elvis Presley and had them hanging at the house – he was commissioned to sell them for Gordon Russell.

He was back once more with Gordon. Gordon's dusty red Cadillac was often in the yard, and Antony would stop whatever he was doing to entertain him. And they would go into the backyard and suck clams and drink beer. Gordon made light of Antony, called him "the frog," and Antony took this as a sign he was once again in that inner circle of people and events where he so wished to be.

By this time Nevin thought of only one thing – of extracting himself from Antony – who had been bullying him for a month.

And yet each time he thought of getting away, new complications arose – new facts were introduced into the complicated arrangements he and Antony had, all of which changed day by day, with Antony's incessant calculations. And each day Nevin was forced to pretend that everything was going along just the way they wished it – and, in fact, nothing was happening that he himself did not foresee.

He did not foresee that he would have to wade up to his arse in water, while Antony waited on the shore, hidden in the bushes when they went to poach salmon.

Nor did he foresee that he would have to wait hours on Antony in places like St. Antoine or Petit Rocher, while Antony would strut about paying no attention to him, chewing on Chiclets.

And each time Nevin went to quit – each time he decided that it was enough – each time one thing drew him back. Something which complicated everything else. Antony made him feel he was ungrateful, that he, Antony, was only trying to make them both money.

"I've one son now who doesn't do anything – lives in a cuddy, kicks the snot out of women, and has no future. I have to support eight people all by myself – and my partner and his wife also."

By day Nevin had the look of certain people of his generation who miscalculated what was significant in the events of their youth – and though still driven by those events, and still assured of their significance, nothing worked so well for them as it did those few years when they were protected by the parents they were so committed to being different from.

But he did not talk about this. He only wanted one thing. Just as in the winter he wanted heat, and last spring he wanted to be paid his money back – now he wanted escape from the heat, the blackflies, and the illegal enterprises Antony was propelling them towards.

He would look at Antony, with his welder's cap, his torn red jacket, his ELVIS LIVES button, and realize that all his ideals had come down to stealing two kegs of swish.

The biggest problem was Vera. How could he admit to her that he had stolen. When Vera asked him how he was doing, or especially if she tried to include him in a joke about Antony, Nevin would turn away.

One morning they took the truck and drove along the upper part of the doctor's land. It was mid-morning. They came to a huge brown puddle. The poplar trees that overhung the roadway were caught in a milky light.

They stopped at the puddle, and were looking for a place to turn – in another instant they would have been gone. But just then a young cow moose and her little calf stepped out on the road. The little mother was not much bigger or older than her offspring. She stood on the far side of the puddle, on the right-hand side of the road near the turn, flicking her ears and waiting for her calf to wobble up behind her.

The calf kept twirling its ears to keep the hundreds of flies off it.

"Get out your side – but don't slam the door," Antony ordered.

"Why?" Nevin said.

"Why – what do you mean why?"

Once Nevin got out, Antony pulled the seat forward and took out his rifle. Nevin was filled with a mixture of fear and excitement.

He heard Antony cursing because he dropped his bullets and had to reach under the truck for them.

By this time the calf had wandered across the puddle and its mother now waited in the centre of the road.

Antony's hands shook as he put the 180-grain bullets in, but his whole body shook as well. And just as he raised the gun, the mother gave a short owl-like call to her child. The calf, instead of heeding this warning, walked even closer, on the left of the road, still twirling its ears, curious as to who they were.

"Why aren't you twirling your ears?" it seemed to ask.

Antony managed to fire once and the gun jammed. But that first shot dropped the cow, and it bellowed, falling ahead on its knees and making a track in the dust at the puddle's edge. Its eyes, to Nevin who had never witnessed anything killed, looked about as if wondering at the nature of its distress.

It called to its calf, a gurgled cry because one of its lungs was filling with blood, and tried to stand up – which it did momentarily – and run – which it couldn't do.

The calf looked back at its mother, and then looked back at the men, and ran behind a bush, where it stood watching, its ears still twirling, one clockwise, one counter-clockwise, over the top of the branches. Now the mother ran also, but fell headlong into the alders.

Antony walked straight into the puddle, still trying to unjam his rifle, and cursing. "Get the axe, Nevin – get the axe," he said.

And Nevin reached into the box of the truck and got the axe.

The cow moose was bleeding a great deal. Spots of bright red blood were all over the road, but a huge amount of dark clotted blood was on the leaves.

All the while the sun beamed through the milky white trees as it had done five minutes before, and three broken branches the little cow was munching on were still wet from its tongue.

"Give me the axe," Antony was saying. "Give me the axe."

Antony was now beside himself, because the nature of the situation had begun to sink in. They were on the dirt road. Anyone might have heard the shot, or someone might pass by. Not only did they have the cow to worry about, but Antony realized they would have to kill the calf as well – and this was just beginning to sink in, as was the water and blood on his pant legs.

"I'll show you!" he roared.

He crashed the blunt side of the axe down upon the cow's head. This made the cow, as small as it was, stand to its feet, and try to back Antony away. But another blow came down upon its skull, and it fell once more.

The calf had come to watch and was standing ten feet behind Nevin.

After a while, Antony came out of the bushes with the axe in his hand. His big belly was jiggling as he walked, his pants were all twisted. He waved the axe and began to chase the calf.

They had to chase the calf back and forth across the puddle, trying to corner it. For ten minutes it eluded them, while refusing to leave the road. But after hitting it a number of times on the back and legs, it fell, crying, and Nevin was able to finish it with a dozen blows to the back and spine.

Each blow purposeful and spotting his cheeks with blood.

After Nevin went home, he shook for three days. Every time he looked at food he would think of the little calf moose twirling its ears.

"Oh, Nevin," Vera would say, "why aren't you eating your supper – you can't expect me to make supper every night and you not eat."

Nevin would look up and see the pork chops on the table and begin to tremble as if he felt cold.

"I'm not hungry – just feed it to the goats."

And he would leave the table and go to bed. He had hardly seen Antony since that day either. Nevin could not look at him without hanging his head.

"Why, why, why did we do that?" he would say to himself. "God, why did you let this happen?"

And he would stare at the walls, and listen as the wind blew and dust rattled the window – for it was a tumultuously hot dry summer – and he would put the pillow over his head.

But all he envisioned when he closed his eyes was the little calf moose trying to run away, and thinking it had outsmarted them once because it turned left instead of right.

So he would open them again, quickly, and stare at the sheet. Like a person suffering a hangover. Moose swam before his eyes, and water and puddles, and little twigs, and voices of sad animals – all seeming to suffer at the exact same instant.

"Why did you let that happen?" he would ask. Nevin, like every other mortal who cried out, cried out to something, though indeterminate, which was far greater than himself.

And the answer came, just as it had come when his first wife left him years before – through, he thought, no fault of his own.

"God either wills or allows."

There was no other answer at all.

What Nevin was most conscious of now was his great love for Vera. Why this seemed so striking in the midst of his failure he did not know.

"You're just filled with energy," Vera would say, smiling, because she confused his condition with energetic excitement and did not know his agony.

And at work, what did he do? He did nothing. He wore his new work gloves that looked ridiculous upon his slight hands, and picked up whatever it was Antony told him to.

So he had no one at all. He thought really of ending his life – but then he thought of how much he would shame his father if he did this. Or he thought that if he did this, people would laugh at him – maybe, he thought, they would refuse to bury him. So perhaps they would have to cremate him.

He was frightened and apologetic and only wanted people to like him.

And no one in the world seemed to like him or care for him – except Margaret, who helped with the goats, and fed the chickens, and made sure the rabbits didn't do too much damage to the garden.

Margaret had no friends. All summer she had been alone, doing her jigsaw puzzle, or taking care of Valerie. Every time they met she would talk about her brother, Ivan. She was sad about him. And worried about him – because of all the rumours. Everyone said things about him. It seemed his old friends were the first to turn on him.

Sometimes, when she met Nevin, she would be wearing an old pair of her brother's cutoffs. She was very pretty. She, like her brother Ivan, had inherited that simple strength that showed in her movement.

Once, when she brought him one of her grandmother's blueberry muffins, she said: "We'll have to go on a picnic."

And once she wanted him to go swimming.

"Where will we meet?" he said.

"I change down behind the shed on the shore," she said. "You could meet me there if you want to."

He only wanted to talk to her and eat muffins, but he kept going over in his mind if this was really the case. He was worried that he had hidden intentions, and therefore had been embarrassed when she mentioned swimming. He had to realize that he was much older than she.

"No, no, no," he said. "I'm not going to see her again."

But then, the next day, she came running over with two pails and told him that if he wanted blueberry muffins, he would have to help her pick some blueberries.

That day he and Antony were supposed to go to Buctouche, but since it was raining Antony didn't want to go. He had decided to stay home and stamp DECEASED on the most pressing bills, and return them – something which never failed to stall those he was indebted to.

Margaret and Nevin met halfway between his house and hers and stood for a while smoking under a spruce tree, which allowed them both to stand as long as they stood with their backs pressed to the trunk. It was where Margaret came to be alone, where she had built a fort. Spruce boughs dropped over them and they could hear the rain beating and pelting the ground, while only one of Nevin's shoulders was getting a little wet.

Nevin started telling her about his early manhood, about university, about the things he and his first wife used to do.

Nevin talked for almost an hour. Margaret was silent, but sometimes her eyes would wander a little, and she became uneasy, and then she would grow attentive again.

After he stopped talking, he looked at her.

"Ivan used to take me out once in a while as he cut pulp," Margaret said. "He could work all day in the rain – or snow. I would have to get under a tree or something – and then I'd get cold, and he'd have to come make me a fire – and rub me down. At night he'd sit me up on Ginger Cake and lead me out. And if we got out before eight o'clock, then he would get me a pop and a bag a chips at Donnie's store. Ivan once had a pit bull that bit me, and he had to destroy it – as soon as he saw me bleeding. That was it for the pit bull."

For some reason it seemed she said this as if answering his story. And in her story there seemed more freedom than his could ever possess. But what was sad is he did not know why.

"I love November eleventh because we would go hunting. Two years ago it was snowing, and Ivan and I sat in a tree from seven in the morning. He didn't get down, and wouldn't let me out of the tree. He wouldn't let me sneeze. Every time I wanted to sneeze he would stick his finger across my nose. He wouldn't let me piss" – Margaret said "piss," which startled Nevin – "so I had to wet my pants – honest. He said to me, 'You

176

wanted a deer – make the best of it – this is my last chance at getting you a deer.'

"The day got longer and snow fell – and he kept checking his sights. We were staring down at a little gully. I had worn leather boots and they were freezing my toes off, but I didn't want to complain – I was afraid if I did Ivan would push me out of the tree." She looked at Nevin and smiled. Now and then rain fell off one of the spruce bellies and landed on her chest. "So we waited. And the snow got badder and badder. It started to blow – and was cold – and Ivan didn't move, didn't speak to me. Every now and then he would take out some scent from a deer's privates and drop it on me head. 'There, you can get yerself a young buck tonight,' he'd whisper." She looked at Nevin again, glancing quickly as she always did.

"We kept on waiting. The day got longer. I was scrunched up beside him. Then I was afraid we wouldn't be able to get out to the road, and be snowed in and die in a ditch somewheres – the snow come down, over my pants – there was six inches of snow on my shoulder."

She stopped talking and lit a cigarette.

"Then it started to get dark – I was getting real scared. I wanted to go home – it weren't no fun. I had chapped my bum from peein myself," she laughed. "It weren't no fun at all. 'It's dark, Ivan,' I said. 'Wait,' Ivan said. So I waited 'cause there was nothing else to do. It was that dark I didn't even see it. It looked like a bush. It was about two hundred yards away. And I was staring at it all along, but not knowing that it was nothing more than a bush. Ivan had seen it for the last fifteen minutes. He hadn't taken his eyes off it. But it had to step out – and he waited. He just stared at it. Suddenly it stepped out and began to walk towards us – covered in snow, with its head up, and its tongue tasting the air. Ivan shot it in the head."

She finished her story. The rain beat down, and she shivered. And Nevin, for the life of him, not knowing why, bent over and kissed her.

She just stared at him, going on with her story.

"Then we had to lug and lug and lug," she said. "It was a 247-pound, 12-point buck – and after he cleaned it up we had to lug it. I was never so tired. I was sorry for the deer, but the only thing I wanted was to get it home and eat its liver," she nodded with conviction. "I never seen a man so small as Ivan so strong."

Nevin, not knowing why, went to kiss her again, but she turned away, and he coughed and backed up.

"I've never been kissed before," she said.

"YOU!" came a voice. It was Antony. "AND YOU – IT'S YOU!"

"No, no, it's not me," Nevin said, weakly. First you could see Antony's boots and pant legs and then his whole large body moving towards them.

"I'll get you," Antony said. "I'll get the police – that's what I'll do."

"NO, NO," Nevin managed. "It's not me."

Margaret had run off the other way towards the house, and Antony was hauling Nevin towards his. "NO – don't tell!"

Vera was standing out in the yard now, with her right hand shading her eyes as she looked in their direction, although it was not sunny, and a goat near the garbage pail stood eating a tuft of blond cabbage while the rain off the roof hit the lid like a drum.

"What's wrong," Vera said. Pregnant, with her feet swollen, her eyes were puffy, and her face bore the

178

expression of all people who in the midst of planning joy come upon sudden upheaval and tragedy.

"He was fondling my daughter's titties."

"I didn't," Nevin said.

But Antony was incensed, with the irrational anger that at times hits broken men when they have found a beacon for rage.

"He was at her – I'm getting the police."

"No, please," Vera said, "don't get the police."

"I'm sorry," Vera said, "I'm sorry." This is all she could say. "I'm sorry," she kept saying, "I'm sorry."

Suddenly Antony turned and walked away, left Vera and Nevin standing beside their little house, in the rain.

Nevin could hear them about the house. He was sure they were about. The next afternoon, as he was sitting in his chair, he saw Antony and Frank Russell walking towards his house, Frank with his left foot turned sideways and his green work shirt making his red hair look fierce in the afternoon heat.

And behind them, at right shoulder, was Jeannie, with a determined nasty grimace, with an unflagging step beside the men.

"Come on out," Antony said.

Frank and Jeannie stood side by side, looking towards the house, the shiniest thing on Frank being his immobile belt buckle in the suffering heat, and Jeannie, her hair, which was a hay-crop red thrust back into a bun, and a small hearing aid in her right ear.

Jeannie looked from one man to the other.

"They want you to go out," Vera said to Nevin, looking out the window at them.

Nevin said nothing.

Vera stared out at the two men and the woman standing in her lane near the row of alders.

"Child molester," Frank yelled.

And Jeannie, with an ever-present nod, looked up at her husband in the blind approval that they had for each other.

Finally, Vera went out and stood at the door. Her maternity top lay on her, and her face bore the expression of suffering and beauty.

"Go away," she said.

"We don't want no problem with you," Antony said. "I always liked you –"

"For my sake," she said.

Vera went back inside and locked the door. She went over and sat beside Nevin.

Nevin laid his head back and said nothing. Then he went to the window, looked out it, and stepped back.

"Are they still there?" Vera said.

He nodded. Then he started walking about the house, with his knapsack, picking things up.

"What are you doing?" Vera said, her hands clasped tightly together so that some parts of her fingers were red and the other parts white, and tears started to run down her face.

"Packing to leave," Nevin said, as if all of this was natural and she should realize it.

"You can't," she said.

She started to cry, and Nevin, not really understanding what he was picking up, or why he had the knapsack in his hands, finally threw it down and went and stood in the corner.

An hour passed and they were in the same position.

"Go look out the window, Vera," Nevin whispered.

There was a smell of cinder in the air, that smell that came from the back of the house on hot days. The goats were in the garden. Vera's pruning shears lay in the dirt where she had dropped them the day before just as she had seen Nevin being dragged across the yard.

Vera stood and went to the window. Yes, they were still there.

She waited by the window, looking at the three of them – to her, they had the weight of a sudden, furious apocalypse.

Nevin was still in the corner, leaning against the wall.

"I'll phone the police," she said, breathing out of her nose quietly.

"No," he said.

"Then what do you want me to do?"

"I don't know," he said. "I don't care." And he sank down against the wall, with his elbows on his knees and his hands dangling outward.

"Then I'll make supper," she said.

The heat bore down, and Vera picked up her vegetables on the fork and ate.

Now and again Nevin would look towards the window and see Jeannie's small face looking in at him. He would look at her and pick up some water and drink. Vera silently continued to eat.

"We got the horse here," Jeannie yelled.

"We'll tear the door off," Frank said.

Vera kept her back rigid in the chair, her eyes on her plate, her fork in her left hand, and her right hand under the tablecloth.

"Gaddup," Jeannie yelled to Rudolf. "Gaddup outta that."

"Gaddup, you son of a whore," Frank yelled.

And Nevin, when he heard this, smiled solemnly.

There was a jerking of a chain, and the whinny of the old half-blind and ill-treated horse. The air was suffocating, more so than before.

There was some confusion in the yard and Nevin got up to look out the window. He couldn't see clearly because of the sun in his eyes, reflected off the water. Vera sat where she was. Nevin went to the window in the far room and looked out. Here he could see Ivan with a pitchfork in his hand, standing between them and the house. He had already unhitched Rudolf and had walked it about, holding it by the halter, which he had slipped over its neck.

"I'm taking the horse back to the shed," Ivan said. Jeannie walked up to grab the halter and Ivan simply pushed her down and, without comment to her, said to Antony, "Leave the yard."

Antony, backing up slightly, stood separated from the other two and watched.

Then he pointed a finger towards the house, but Ivan never looked his way.

"Yer some big-feelinged, arentcha," Frank said. "I'll have to take you down a peg or two."

"As I said before – don't let fear stop you," Ivan said, holding the fork to his throat.

Nevin couldn't tell what other things were said. But no more altercation arose.

He kept going from one window to the other to listen. But he only got bits and pieces.

Finally Antony went away and, with him, Frank. Jeannie was the last to go, her black, red-topped rubber boots looking sorrowful in the heat, staring over her shoulder at Ivan as she walked.

By the time Nevin came downstairs and opened the door, Ivan was leading the horse out of the yard behind the shed, the horse moving solemnly into the brush. Nevin yelled to him to come back but Ivan didn't hear – or, at any rate, he didn't turn around.

13

Antony's story was the same one at all times. It was just presented differently, with an indefinable self-deception and a lasting hope that the best points in it were true. And it had become clear now that his side lay with people who had made light of him, ridiculed his family, cheated him out of money, defamed his wife, bore false witness to his son, and held him in contempt.

For the moment, he was satisfied. He felt he'd gotten back at almost everyone in the world.

"Well – I'm well out of that," he said to Ivan, as Ivan brought the horse about in the dooryard. "You're right, there – I shouldn't get mixed up with Nevin – and all that crew."

Ivan looked at him and didn't speak.

"Nevin and Vera are the worst set of Walloons I ever saw," Antony said. "With all that hypocrite stuff." He looked at Ivan and sighed. He was sitting on a bale of hay in the dark side of the shed. Far away, other sounds could be made out in the early evening, the passing of a car and the starting of a chain saw.

"And besides," Antony said, "look what they did for you – Vera and Nevin didn't do you any favours either, Ivan – let me tell you that. So I told Frank and Jeannie I'm not going down there and start up anything, but then I figured I had as much right there as anyone else – take when Gloria left. Clay Everette had me on the road day and night driving grader so they could be together, and everyone knowed about it except me – and everyone knowed when I was out ploughing they'd be together. So when I found out – for four months I didn't even quit my job – I just kept going, pretending also that I hadn't yet found out."

He looked at Ivan and said nothing for a second. He seemed genuinely sad at this.

"And then I was beaten up that time – had the snot pounded out of me by people up in town that night there – 'member that?

"So anyway, now it's Nevin and Margaret, and I just went crazy – I shoulda realized it, right from the start.

"And Vera, too, had a big black attack over at the university there with some Watutsi – mark my words on that – skinny as a hen's cunt back then, big shoulders, looked like Ralphie, almost the same sex eighty per cent of the time – to think that we went and fought off the Norman's for that crew there.

"None of them were any favourite friend of yers in this here scrape with Cindi, Ivan. The whole crew would rather sit back in their houses and twick the hairs off their arse before they'd move to help you. And then Cindi gets into the big aborted scrape down river. If you ask me about it – we could have called the kid Lemondo or something like that – I figured Lemondo after your great-uncle Lemondo."

Ivan was brushing the horse and looking at the

sores on its back, dug deep and filled with dirt, and its mouth ran a purple phlegm. Far in the corner, back beyond the fox bins, was Rudolf the red-nosed reindeer's painted sled, with its runners coated with sawdust.

"So we're well out of that there, all of them. Fall is coming soon and, mark my words, they'll all want you back again to shape up the sleigh trails for their sleigh rides, and turn the horses out and wash down the stall all the time – and give those little twats their riding lessons –"

"But they didn't take no one else to court, did they – except you – and it was all in Ruby's head to get Cindi with Dorval Gene and have her to go with him – it was just a whim – something to do for the summer. So now summer is getting on, and there's this big tickedy boo going on between Dorval and Ruby."

"And," Antony said, "where was Ralphie when you needed him?"

"Will you shut your mouth please, Antony?"

"Hear Ralphie came to you to get the money back for Nevin – some ironic, if you ask me about the whole thing. That is, he put you and your father against one another for the first time in their life –"

Ivan turned and looked at his father, and then in fury he punched the poor horse in the head and turned and left the stall.

"Oh, sure," Antony yelled. "Beat up on the horse, beat up on me, beat up on Jeannie Russell, beat up on yer wife, beat up on us all – but you won't listen to the truth of the problem – will you!"

And he followed his son outside into the light, across the yard, screaming at him to come back, and for some reason, crying.

No one knew where he was. Ivan didn't tell even Margaret, who was the last person he saw before he left.

The nights were still soft and warm, though there was a hint of frost. The trees sat heavy in the dark – the highway bathed in yellow light, the field strangely mistlike in the moonlight.

He slept half the day, and at dark, lit a fire, after the sun went down, cooked some fish in flour, boiled tea and potatoes, and ate. Then he would move down through the woods, following the coyote he had promised to trap for Olive and Gerald. As he had told them, he didn't want to kill her, but if she was coming out near the child, he would.

At three in the morning, he would be sitting on the same stump he circled to every night, smoking a cigarette, listening to the wind move down through the trees. He would smoke two or three cigarettes at the same spot, and then he would move down through the woods again, and back to his camp.

He would lie back, and listen to the wind, and with dawn he would drift away to sleep.

He kept this up for four nights. On his fifth night, just before he was about to go back to his camp, he heard the coyote in among some spruce, where he had set his traps. He realized the coyote had got caught and was dragging the poplar pole the trap was attached to down to the river.

Ivan waited until dawn before he began to track her. The old coyote was smart, but she had her pups with her, and was easily followed because of the pole she had to drag.

She was caught by her right hind leg – and she had attempted to chew the leg when the pole had become wedged between two windfalls. But she had managed to drag herself under the trees without getting caught up, and continued her desperate course, with her little ones yelping encouragement.

She ran, she hid, she manoeuvred, she lay down, with only her ears up. She bit at the trap, the pole, and her leg. And always Ivan came closer.

Ivan had no rifle with him. He had his buck knife and a club of wood he had picked up along the way, banging it against a tree to make sure it wasn't rotted.

Then he came to a clearing. It was small, and tangled all round with nettles and waist-high grasses – and he lost the trail. Ivan was now sweating in the morning sun. Sweat clung to his face and opened shirt, and dripped from his nose and fell on his chest. In behind him was Hennessey's swamp – so named because it cut the farthest side of Dr. Hennessey's property. There was an old bridge built over this swamp that had not been used in forty years. It was made of poplar poles and looked like ripped-up shreds of tar.

Ivan took out his compass, and, flicking his right hand against his ears to keep the mosquitoes away – while dozens of them sucked at the very hand he waved – he took a reading, realizing that the coyote had been backtracking for some time. He put his compass in his vest pocket. He had on a fishing vest, because he could carry everything he needed in it, and he looked about.

On the other side of the swamp, rising out of the ghosting mist, was a maple tree, which Ivan caught out of the corner of his eye, and, cutting along the edge of

188

the swamp, he made it over and climbed it. He climbed it easily, and when he got three-quarters of the way up, he sat on a branch and looked around. He looked for ten to fifteen minutes without seeing a thing, and was actually drifting off to sleep. And then, in a half-conscious shrug, he opened his eyes and saw a pair of eyes blink ten yards away, looking up at him. She had been there all the time, deep in the nettles, not moving.

As soon as she knew she had been spotted, and though the pole was very heavy, she turned quickly towards the river.

Ivan went to step onto a lower branch, but was so busy watching her he missed it and fell twenty feet.

He landed on his side. But he was up on his feet in a moment, and though it took him ten minutes to get a good breath of air, and though he vomited, he was furious now with the coyote, and remorseless.

He moved forward through the now hip-high nettles, clutching his side.

The coyote moved quickly, in spite of her burden and her pups, whom she was continually watching, and who barked in front of her.

Down they went into the spruce, past the old McDurmot property – where a house stood from 1887-1941 – along the alders, through the stands of poplar and maple, into the fir, into the gully, where the sound of the river became clear.

And Ivan, clutching his side, and leaning against trees every now and then, followed them.

The pups were the first to the river, but halted as soon as they got to the water, looking back as the female dragged the pole down over the bank, and then sat quickly on her haunches to bite at the trap. It

was a hot morning and there was a mist of bugs float-
ing above the brown water. A red bird sat on a red rock
in the middle – and to the female coyote's misfortune,
a porter was working the far side of the river.

She heard the loud banging, sniffed the air, howled
to her pups, and turned to face Ivan.

Ivan watched her a moment. He had lost his club
and looked for another, couldn't find any, and
stepped out.

She turned one way along the shore, and then the
other – howled, bared her teeth at him – continually
watching for her pups, who, whimpering, darted in
and out of the woods.

Ivan got behind her, picked the pole up and hauled
it towards him, with his buck knife out. But as things
would have it, he banged his sore side with the pole,
felt a terrible pain, and fell to his knees. The coyote
was over him then, and he only managed to get an arm
out or she would have slashed his throat.

She bit through to the bone in his left arm, but he
picked her up while he stood and drove the knife
deep into her brain.

She fell as if she had never lived, and yet as if her
whole life had been preparing for this death. There
were some ticks in her ears, as if they shared a common mystery with her, and some fresh nettles in her
tail. Her teats were still milky. Her eyes watered. A
clover was stuck in between the pads of her right
forepaw.

Ivan was bleeding very badly, so he tore his shirt and
tried to tie a tourniquet. He made his way up along
the bank, feeling again as if he had to vomit. He had
a five-mile walk to the road. It took him the rest of
the day.

He rested on an upstairs cot in his grandfather Allain's house for almost a day and a half without telling anyone he was injured.

He kept drifting in and out of sleep. He ran a temperature, vomited some more, kept waking up to look at his left arm. The mattress and the pillow slip were soaked in blood.

Some time during the second night, Margaret came in to speak to him. He was in the smallest room, with the slanted walls and the stovepipe, and the window looking down to the bay.

Everything in this room was part of his life. The wallpaper he'd helped his grandmother with, the furniture he and Antony had bought. A picture of Ralphie at Heath Steele Mines, which he had given Ivan – he had written on the back, "To Ivan, in friendship." There was also a picture of Gloria when she graduated at eighteen – his mother, young and fastidious. An old scrapbook from the 1950s that had belonged to someone he didn't know – who had moved away some time ago – and left nothing but pictures that had no dates or titles. These were pictures he had often looked at. One was of a swimming pool at a hotel in Florida, with some people sitting on deck chairs, about 1960.

"Who the fuck would they be?" he would often say, walking about the house, scratching his head. "Hey," he would yell to his grandmother, "oh, deaf one –"

"What, darlin?"

"Were you ever in Florida, sitting on a deck chair?"

"Of course not – I haven't even been to Bathurst."

"Well, who took this picture?" he would say, rubbing his nose and looking at it.

Sometimes he felt he must be trying to make the ceiling revolve, just to pretend he was ill – but then it actually whirled in circles and seemed to draw him closer to it, and then he would vomit.

Yes, there were other times too. They would go to the church picnic. He would always be kicked out of the church picnic. No matter how he dressed, or tried to look – that is, he tried to dress and look exactly the same as everyone else who was on their way down to the picnic – he would end up being kicked out of the picnic by one of the priests.

He would come home, sit on the doorstep, smoking cigarettes and listening to the grasshoppers tick in the yard, with a heavy pair of black shoes still smelling of the nice polish he'd put to them.

Then his mother would be driven home by Clay Everette – whom he only knew then as Mr. Madgill.

"Every goddamn year," Gloria would say, grabbing him by the ear, and dragging him squealing into the house, "you get kicked out of the picnic –"

"I know," he would say, "I know. I try to turn over a new leaf, I do. Next year I'll kick the shit out of the priest – let go of my ear."

Then he remembered the nights in January. The snow would be high, and the sky clear as a bell. Little girls – there was always a bunch at the house – sat on the porch to see their breath so they could all pretend they were smoking, and the chunks of snow left on the road by the grader felt unpleasant under your boots.

He remembered his father coming home late at night – and when he opened the door he brought the glittering cold in with him on his skin. He would smile and hand Ivan an apple. There would be chunks of maple burning in the stove.

Of course, it wasn't his father at all – it was Margaret, washing his arm, and the facecloth had become red with dried blood.

She lifted him up with her left arm, and held him against her breast to see where he'd cut his head open in the fall. Ivan hadn't remembered anything about cutting his head open. He only remembered he thought there was more blood than there should be from the coyote bite and that he had gotten very dizzy when he climbed the hill.

Then there was the time he stole three cars in one night – and drove them about, but got caught because when he took them back he parked them in the wrong driveways. The next day a lady from the Children's Aid and a police constable took him from one house to the next.

"The Ford is supposed to be parked here – not the Datsun."

"Is that right?" Ivan said. "How did they get mixed up –"

"How did you do that?" the lady asked.

"I didn't – the coyote did," he said.

Margaret had lain him back on the cot, and he answered her. She spoke French and he answered her in French.

It seemed important that he tell her something – but she had left the room.

Margaret ran downstairs, facecloth in hand, and began to wash it. She went back up and sat beside her brother for almost two hours, and then went downstairs to check the time. It was two in the morning, and the wind was cool, the sky dark, and she could hear a bird screech somewhere. She did not know if she should phone an ambulance or not, and when she went back upstairs she saw Ivan sitting up in bed, trying to light a cigarette. He had loosened his pants and had his shirt off, so she could see all the marks on him – not only from his fall, but from other things as well.

He looked up at her, dragged on his cigarette, and then leaned back to look under the curtain at the night.

"What time is it?" he asked.

"Two or something," Margaret said. "I'll phone the hospital."

"I don't need any hospital – where is everybody?"

"In bed –"

"Two in the morning –" Ivan said.

"Yes, it's dark out."

Ivan nodded as if in a daze and dragged from his smoke again, then looked over at his boots.

"What's on TV?" he said.

"Nothing – it's off the air."

Ivan had forgotten that though he could get cable just five miles away, Margaret was unable to.

Then he asked her to make him something to eat, and got to his feet.

"I need an ice pack for me head too," he smiled.

"What do you want to eat?" Margaret asked.

"Bacon," he said. He could smell frost on the dark sill, and in the air about the pictures, and in the air near the flower pot filled with dry soil and a plant that hadn't grown.

Now he sat in the kitchen and looked at his arm and chest. His chest had been scraped almost raw in the fall, his rib cage on his left side was blueish yellow. "Where's Dad?"

"Down river."

Ivan said nothing.

"You probably need a tetanus shot for your arm," Margaret said to him.

"Probably," he said, looking at it and shaking his head.

"So," he said, "how was yer summer there, Maggie Muggins?"

"I didn't do too much," she spoke as she worked, making noise with the dishes and frying pan, as if she wasn't certain of what she was saying. She didn't mention Nevin. "I saved money for the Exhibition," she said, "and Cindi said she would take me." She didn't look at him, she looked at the stove. "I asked her if you could come too – and she didn't say no," she said, as if an afterthought. But still she didn't look his way.

He didn't answer. He didn't feel like eating either. His head seemed to be numb, and he felt like he might get sick again.

"But I didn't say yes or no to anything," Margaret said. "I bought a belt, too – you want to see it?"

She went inside, and got the belt from the closet.

"It was for when I go to the Exhibition," she said, as always when she tried to be grown-up she sounded like a little girl.

He smiled at her for a long time, and at the belt in her hands.

Then, after trying to eat some bacon and eggs, he went back to the room and fell asleep almost at once.

He slept for another day.

Cindi had begun to realize the shifting attitudes. Ruby now no longer saw Dr. Savard – whom she had been "totally" in love with – and she and Dorval Gene had had that falling out which usually happens to conspirators – even when they only realize the nature of their conspiring in hindsight, and still believe in its purpose.

It tumbled all over her at once and troubled her.

Also, Cindi was beginning to see that everything had been done on a whim – that if, for instance, Ruby wasn't in love with Armand, it might not have happened, or if Armand wasn't agitated by that case where the woman was sent to Moncton, it might not have happened. It might not have happened if she and Dorval Gene had stood up to Ruby – who wanted them to pretend that they were in the depths of that inner circle, simply because she was in love with Armand and had written his name on a stall.

By now everyone had tired of it. No one cared about Cindi. She was almost completely forgotten. Part of this was because there were other events which usurped her.

When weeks before she was the most high-profile person she had ever been, no one paid attention to her any more. The old doctor still dropped in now and again. Margaret came over to visit, and Adele still came down once a week.

Every time the doctor came in he would talk roughly, say too much, and be sorry for it. Then he would ask her if she had seen Ivan.

"No one's seen him at all," Cindi would say. She would sigh as if she was as puzzled as everyone else.

He would look down at her, then shuffle across to the refrigerator and look into it – to make sure that she had enough food – but really to make sure that she was eating food at all.

"I think he just went way up into the woods," Hennessey said one day, almost fondly, as he leaned against the fridge to make it close.

"Maybe," Cindi answered.

Finally Cindi went out of the apartment.

It was a bright cool day in August, so she wore a sweater that came down over her shorts. Half her toes were painted red, the other half were painted green – she liked to mix them up, every second toe.

Her hair was piled loosely on her head with pins, so that it lifted upwards from her ears. She walked with the characteristic wiggle she always had, a wiggle that was almost unnoticeable but gave a curious and wonderful sensuality to her movement that had attracted far more men than one might, at first, suppose. She had put some blush on her cheeks and did her eyelashes while she stood outside in the sun. A little boy – Harvey LeBlanc, he was called – went around and around her with his tricycle, taking shots at her with a water pistol.

She lit a cigarette and walked down the road, holding the cigarette outward at her right hip.

There was a smell of manure and hay, and the tick, tick of grass. The bay was blue, and so were the trees in the distance.

Cindi found Ruby in the barn with Tantramar. Ivan had told her not to jump with Tantramar when he wasn't there, but she had the jumps set up, and was leading the horse out into the arena with the crop in her left hand.

Cindi was not allowed to go near any of the horses in the upper stalls. Tantramar was one. It was Ruby's horse. Anything that was Ruby's one was not allowed to touch. Except for her father, who continually took things away from her – like her credit cards – and then gave them back twofold. That was how she got the colt. He took Tantramar away from her and then let her have Tantramar back, and bought her a colt.

Cindi stood for a long time without being noticed. Ruby tightened the girth and tried to get a boot into the stirrup, as the horse moved in a very slow circle around her. She was wearing dark tight breeches and big black boots.

"Will you settle the fuck down," Ruby said. She was so beautiful. No wonder so many loved her.

"Ruby –"

Ruby turned about and looked at her. The horse gave a snort.

"I'm sorry," Cindi said, "for the trouble I caused." And then, taking a breath, she said, "I want you to forgive me."

"Don't worry about it," Ruby said, looking over at her.

"I caused a lot of trouble for everyone," Cindi said.

"Who doesn't?" Ruby said, walking Tantramar to the box so she could get into the saddle.

"I guess we all do at times," Cindi said, smiling faintly.

"Uh huh," Ruby said, checking the length of the stirrups – as if this suddenly showed that she knew she had been betrayed.

"How's Dorval?" Cindi said.

"Dorval who? Don't mention that cocksucking backstabber to me – he's gone home to Montreal."

Then, after saying this, and as if this action, too, showed that everyone she knew and helped had disappointed her, she shortened her contact, snapped the crop, and sent Tantramar around the outside rail at a canter.

When she looked back towards the arena door, Cindi was gone. She brought the horse back to a trot and patted its glossy neck.

When Cindi left the barn, Margaret, who was standing near the paddock fence, called her over to tell her about Ivan.

When Ivan woke, it was glowing red twilight. She was sitting in the corner, with a fruit basket in her hands, looking at him.

She had worn her blue dress, the one she had bought in Moncton, and she was wearing a tam on her head. She had combed her hair so it fell straight down across her ears, and she had a small heart-shaped pendant about her neck. That is, she looked totally different than he had ever seen her look before. The plastic was pulled across the top of the fruit basket so stiffly that it seemed to make her air more formal.

"Hello, Ivan," she said. She smiled, just slightly. "Here," she said, handing him the basket – and it was done so abruptly she almost let it drop on the floor.

"And I've got you a card – now where is that card?" She began looking through her purse. "Where is that card – I got it – where –" As she looked for the card she glanced at him, trying to smile, and then looked quickly into her purse.

"Here," she said, hauling it out. "Of course it says, 'I hope all the nurses are pretty,' but there are no nurses here, so you'll have to imagine nurses." Again she smiled and then looked about.

He looked at the card and basket, and watched her. There were some last slivers of light, and then they paled away. Car lights from the highway flickered into the room as they passed, and every time the car lights passed he could see the little heart-shaped pendant around her neck.

Every now and then she would look at him, and smile in a frightened way, and look around the room again.

"Is that Ralphie's picture there?" she said.

He nodded.

Though it was dark, she picked it up for a moment and looked at it. She didn't know what to do, so she put the picture back, rubbing her hand along its frame.

"He's a good friend to give you that picture," she said, as if she were talking to a child.

He nodded, but she did not see his nod.

"He's a good friend," Cindi said again, as a person will to comfort herself when her statement has not been answered.

Then a sudden dreadful silence came upon them both for a long time.

She sat on the far edge of the bed and didn't look his way.

When he woke up much later, she was still sitting there. And, as always with her, she could tell that he was awake.

"Are we gonna go home tomorrow?" he said.

14

They were making other plans. By the last of August they had their apartment cleared out, the bags and boxes packed, and were ready to leave.

First they were going to Kingston, and then on to Sudbury, where one of Ivan's uncles worked and had promised him a job if he could get there by the end of September.

At the last moment they decided to send their belongings by freight on to Sudbury, take the train to Kingston, and buy a car there.

Ivan had gone to the wharf, had taken the little dog to Cindi's mother and asked her to keep it, and he would send for it when they settled. He had met Frank and Jeannie Russell one day as he walked along the road. They were walking towards him. They didn't speak until the last moment, and then in a litany of outrage at the boys on the road who were bothering their mackerel nets, asking him if he'd seen any of them, and looking at him as if he would understand their complaints against all others who made the mistake of living.

"I haven't seen no one about today," he said.

"Young ones on the road," Jeannie said, sniffing and looking up at him with a dour expression.

"Some big-feelinged lads," Frank said, as his wife looked up at him.

There was a silence.

"Mr. Big-feelinged Lads," Frank said and they moved slowly away, cutting down the wagon road and into the stubby field near their house, Jeannie walking behind him, her movement in her square red jacket somehow totally womanly.

"Do you want to invite Adele and Ralphie down for supper before we go away?" Cindi asked.

There was a long pause.

"No," he said.

Adele, finding out that they were going, invited them up to the house. But at the last moment Ivan, who was ready to go, couldn't bring himself to go. He sat near the kitchen table, in his new corduroy pants and nylon jacket, looking now and again at the clock on the wall, and looking away from it as if the time caused him pain.

Olive came by with money because he had spent his time to trap the coyote, but he didn't want the money, and so refused to take it – and this made him feel sad for her. She was a small woman with black hair and oyster-coloured skin.

"Well, you saved us a lot of worry at any rate," she said.

"Oh, they weren't doing too much, those fellas – just out about," he said, smiling. Then he lowered his eyes and looked away.

There was a party hastily arranged for them at Allain's, and they went down.

Antony wasn't there. He was in Lemec at this time. So Ivan didn't get to see him.

It seemed to everyone in the house that they were just leaving after their marriage – and that there was going to be a new start to everything.

Their wedding had taken place two years ago. Everyone got drunk and Cindi was kidnapped. They put her in a shed, and then forgot where they had taken her, leaving her there for three hours alone, singing her lungs out. They had Kentucky-fried chicken and had toasted the bride with Golden Nut wine. Then they all had to go out and try to find the bride, late at night checking sheds and barns, and calling her name in the dark along the road.

The day before they were to leave for the train station, Cindi asked Ivan to take two pie plates back to his grandmother.

The woods behind his grandfather's, to the left of the road, was ablaze – there was a good black smoke rising over the trees about three miles away.

When he went into the house, Valerie was busy making herself breakfast as nonchalant as anyone. There was already a haze in the porch, and a smell, as of an old tire.

"Where's Dad?" he said.

"He took Rudolf and went into the woods last night. I think he went poaching salmon," she said, as nondescript as always.

"Ya – and he went in and lit a fire so he could get hired by the forestry to put it out – another make-work project for himself," Ivan said, looking towards the trees.

Valerie went over and looked towards the trees also, sniffed, and said nothing.

"It's likely this is what the old man did," Ivan said. patting her once on the head.

"Pretty likely," Valerie said.

This was not an entirely new phenomenon with Antony. He had discovered this ability to light fires a while ago. He had always complained to Ivan that it was after his marriage had broken up and he was out of work. He had come home from visiting his friends in the north of the province, and found that they did this almost every summer. He began to do it, now and again, himself.

Although Ivan couldn't be 100 per cent positive it was Antony's fire, he couldn't think of any other way it had started.

"I gotta get to the train," he said. "I can't be fuckin about with this all day –"

"No, you can't be fuckin about with this," Valerie said.

"Watch yer mouth," he said. "Jesus Christ, Valerie."

Then he went out and looked into the shed. Rudolf was gone all right. He looked in its stall, saw where it had breathed the last of the dusty oats about in the box, where it had tried to place the hay under it to lay down – just as it had always done. He saw two of its shoes in the corner near the fox mash.

Ivan looked about and picked up a chain lying on the floor and threw it across a beam and started out. Margaret was in the yard.

"Did you see the fire back there?" she said.

Ivan looked up at the trees and nodded matter-of-factly.

"I think the wind is blowing away from us though – don't you?"

Ivan wetted his finger and stuck it into the air as he passed her, so that she laughed.

"I don't think there's any wind at all at the moment," he said.

Margaret had come from her swim and was wearing her black bathing suit. Her skin was covered with goose bumps. She was in bare feet, some dirt had caught on the back of her right leg, and the air smelled hazy.

"Where are you going?" she said.

He turned quickly and kissed her.

"To Sudbury," he said.

"I know that! But I want to show you my jigsaw puzzle first."

So he walked up the stairs and into her bedroom, where half of her room had been taken over by two card tables, upon which a huge jigsaw puzzle lay. It was a winter panorama, but one piece was missing. She had searched her room for days.

"Well – that's too bad," Ivan said.

"Well – I was going to get it put up on the wall, but I won't if I can't find the piece," she said. "It took me five weeks."

They both looked at the puzzle glumly, as if, because of that one piece, they held something against it.

She began to dry her hair with a towel, and it suddenly struck him as very womanly the way she did this.

Just then he heard a voice downstairs. Antony had come home.

"Ivan," he said.

"I'm up here," Ivan said.

Antony moved slowly up the stairs, breathing heavily and clomping along the hallway, banging on his father's door as he passed.

"Fire," he said.

He came to Margaret's door and looked in at them. He was covered in mud and dirt.

"Fire," he said, shaking his head. "There's a fire."

"I know," Ivan said.

"Well, aren't you going to do something about it?"

"No," Ivan said, "I'm going to Sudbury."

"Oh, look," Antony said suddenly, "you've got yer puzzle done –"

"I have it all together but I can't find one piece," she said.

"Oh," Antony said. Then he sniffed and rubbed his hand across his head. "You mean this," he said, going over to the puzzle and taking the piece out of his pocket. "Oh my God – look, it fits," he said, sniffing and scratching his bum.

"You hid it on me," Margaret said. And Antony winked and laughed.

Just then Ivan asked where Rudolf was. Antony admired the puzzle for a moment and then shook his head.

"Where's Rudolf?" Ivan asked a second time.

Antony moved his head, and said, "Oh, he got all caught up on the bridge there and fell into the swamp. I tried for an hour to get him out – but he won't come."

"He's stuck there in the goddamn fire?" Ivan said.

"I tried oats," Antony said, taking some oats out of his pocket, as if "I tried oats" proved beyond a shadow of a doubt that he had done all that was humanly possible.

Ivan turned and walked out the door.

"Well, where the hell are you going?" Antony said, still holding the oats in his hand.

"I'm going to get Rudolf," Ivan said.

Antony then got agitated. "The trouble is the sleigh is there and the lumber," Antony said.

"The sleigh in August? He can't haul a sleigh!"

"Well, what are you going to do?" Antony said in a reasonable voice. "You gonna let that lumber burn –"

"What lumber?"

"Oh, who knows what lumber – it was just lying there."

"That's Dr. Hennessey's lumber," Ivan said.

Antony then took the flat of his right thumb and rubbed the inside of his right nostril, while looking with his big brown eyes at his son.

Ivan shook his head.

"Well – I gotta see about getting this fire fought – I can't stand about all day looking after an old horse," Antony said.

Ivan went towards the door. Antony followed him and Margaret followed Antony.

At the last moment Antony got in an argument with the forestry over how much he would be paid and decided not to trouble himself working the fire. He had lit the fire, he believed, because the night before Gordon had ignored him at the Portage Restaurant, and he felt once again outside that circle of events and people he so wished to be included into. They had all gone to the restaurant, and Antony had to sit at a corner, and ask for a knife and fork. Gordon teased him about this – and Antony kept trying to be included in the conversation about the snow-crab industry in Lemec – as if this conversation and his inclusion into it was the one important yardstick by which everything else was measured. Gordon and his friends ignored him for the most part, and Antony ordered a salad because others had also, wearing his ELVIS LIVES button on his black welder's cap.

✚ ✚ ✚

The woods to the left of his grandfather's house was dry and warm. Ivan could smell sun on his jacket and the faint tang of smoke far away.

He walked straight through the woods and hit the road about an hour later.

He walked along the road, stepping gingerly here and there, moving from one side to the other, looking up at the trees for a sign of wind.

After almost an hour on the road he reached the giant puddle, where Nevin and Antony had encountered the moose the month before, and turned briskly to his right, heading through the trees. Within twenty minutes he was at the fringe of the bog. Far across the bog was the maple tree that he had fallen from.

The sleigh was tipped over and lying on the horse's right-hand side, with one of the runners touching the horse's withers. It had gone off the bridge where half the lumber still sat.

"Oats," Ivan said.

The woods was quiet. Some crows flew south high above him. Up in the tree he was standing under, a small grey squirrel chattered, sucked, and whistled, its body trembling.

"Oats," Ivan said again, shaking his head.

Then he said, "*Plus de fuss*," which is what Antony said whenever he was in trouble.

"*Plus de fuss tout le temps*," he said, and he sat down and lit a cigarette.

Old Rudolf had exhausted his strength trying to get back up on the bridge, trying to escape the sleigh and the stab of the runner, trying to move forward as Antony had coaxed and beaten him – first with his fist, and then with a switch he had cut, but all to no avail. Now the animal was looking gloomily about, now and again trying to bite at some deerflies.

The water in the bog rippled with a breeze that ran from the north towards where Ivan was sitting.

Ivan then butted his cigarette, and then, yanking the belt on his new corduroy pants tighter, he found a suitable place, and started across the bog towards the horse.

✛   ✛   ✛

By the time water tankers got down, the fire had cut the dirt road at two places, burning over an old burn to the left of the bog, and going away from it.

People on the highway had already pulled over in their cars to watch the smoke, and then, as men in trucks started back towards it, they could see the first flames, fanned by a small late-summer breeze hitting the air.

One person who saw the smoke was Vera. She was hanging out her wash, standing in heavy black shoes with red socks, and she could see the trail of smoke that whiskered up over the trees.

But she didn't know what it was. Adele and Ralphie, who were down to see her, told her it had to be a fire.

"Are you sure?"

"Couldn't be anything else," Adele said and then shrugged.

Vera had invited them down because she didn't want to be alone with Nevin – though she had not told them this. Every time Nevin said or did anything she would smile as usual, yet this smile, which was the same as always, seemed to betray everything.

"Good," Nevin said, when he heard the news, "I hope we all burn down."

Vera, in those heavy black shoes with red socks, walked across the room to open up the drapes.

"I think it's burning away from us anyway," she said in a very certain voice, her cheeks fatter because of the pregnancy and her eyes squinting.

"Well, I hope it turns around soon and starts towards us," Nevin said.

Ralphie then left the house, and in a few minutes they could hear him up on the roof, walking about. Nevin went outside and sat on a sawhorse in the long grass near their back shed, looking up at him.

"Can you see it?"

"Oh ya – it's pretty big – want to come up?"

Nevin smiled, jumped to his feet, walked over to the oil barrel, and went to take Ralphie's hand – Ralphie was leaning over the roof edge, as easy as could be.

"Na – never mind," Nevin said, and he went and sat on the sawhorse again.

An hour passed as Ralphie watched the sky.

"How is it now?" Nevin asked.

"Not too good – but I can't tell which way it's burning. Oh listen, here comes a water bomber. Oh look –

that big pine – no, the pine behind it is burning –
water bomber dropped its load too soon – no – well,
here comes another one."

"Ah," Nevin said, "once you've seen one fire, you've
just about seen them all, I figure?"

But already, even though he was miles away from it,
Nevin was already worried about dying in it – and
secretly wanted to run away.

The sky was darkening. There was a low cloud hanging along the side of ditches on both sides of the main
highway and it had the smell of burning leaves. Down
the highway from Garrett's, a moose wandered out
and stood still, watching the traffic. Then it moved
across and into the woods on the other side. A water
bomber scared it, and it went at a run into the bushes.

There was no thought of evacuating any houses
above Garrett's. But down below them, below Oyster
River, the fire had run almost to the bridge, and three
families had left their houses and were standing in
their yards with water hoses.

Antony was now standing out alongside the highway, near his yard, much the way he did in the spring
when Valerie sold her worms. People pulled over in
their cars to talk, and Antony would give advice.

"Can we get down to Oak Point?"

"Sure, just take it slow – there's not much more than
smoke. Turn your lights on – it's not a big fire – just a
little one. A lot a smoke – the wind's sinful though."

Then a forestry half-ton pulled up and the driver
said in a joyful voice that fires sometimes give people,
"You coming with us, Antony?"

211

"No, I got sore feet," Antony said. "I worked all night."

"You probably lit her, did you?" the young boy on the passenger side said as a joke. But Antony glared at him with a terrible ferociousness, and the boy looked guiltily out of the cab window.

"Don't say that on this side of the river," Antony said, because the youngster was from Napan. "Save that there talk for Black River – right, Terry?" he said to the driver.

After the truck left he hobbled back into his yard, picked up the same block of wood he had picked up two months earlier, and threw it into the bushes. Then he walked into the shed. He sat down among his few yapping foxes and drank, looking at Rudolf's old shoes.

✤　✤　✤

Still everything was going normally at Vera's. Even little Cora and Rosie showed up for their piano lesson, just as they were scheduled.

"You can't give them piano lessons," Nevin said. He was getting more and more agitated.

However the little girls were seated across from each other in the piano room, hiding their hands. And Vera was walking about, with the scissors.

"Who's first?" she said.

"Cora," Rosie said.

"Rosie," Cora said.

"I'll go first," Rosie said, holding out her fingers.

"No, I will," Cora said, holding out hers.

And Vera looked from one to the other, snipping the air with her pair of scissors.

"You," Vera said to Cora, grabbing her left hand and cutting her nails. "Now the right."

After Cora was done she walked about the room, something like a little disembodied soul, looking at her fingers to see how close the nails had been clipped, while Rosie, whose operation had not yet begun, cringed and closed her eyes.

Every time Nevin went outside he smelled smoke, saw the darkening air, looked at the bay water, which looked sludgy and white, and felt that none of them were doing the right things. They should all be going somewhere.

He walked outside and shouted up at Ralphie: "How is it, now –"

"I don't know – it hasn't crossed the road yet."

"Well, I want to take some things out of the house."

"Where will you put them?"

"We'll pile them in the field. Come on, snap to it, let's go."

And Ralphie stood, walked across the roof as if he were wearing some type of magnets on his boots, and grabbed on to the eaves, and swung down onto the oil barrel.

When they walked inside, the tick, tick could be heard from the metronome, and every now and then Vera would slap a page with her pointer.

"Da, da, da," she would say. "Listen." And, standing above the little girls, and playing with the fingers of her right hand, she would show them where they were getting mixed up.

"We're taking the piano," Nevin said, coming into the music room. "Everyone out."

And with that Nevin started his day of panic and alarm, which for the life of him he could not control, and like all panic-stricken people he was propelled by some force to start panic in others.

✢   ✢   ✢

Ivan had now climbed upon Rudolf's back and slid forward to its head, trying to unhook the sleigh as he did so, his pants soaked in mud.

The old horse, with its bobbed tail, old studded collar, and twisted blinkers, with two tiny Canadian flags sticking from them, looked back at him. It put its ears back, as Ivan urged it forward, while deerflies and mooseflies landed in the sores the old studded collar had made.

Rudolf, as always, tried to obey, as it did when it hauled thirty kids up the snowy roads, with antlers stuck upon its head, and icicles growing on its mouth, while every time it slipped on its uncleated shoes, the children would roar and laugh, and Santa would slap it forward with a switch.

But when Ivan kicked it, it didn't even bother to move. The sleigh was sideways, the wiffle tree jarred, and its left hind leg was caught. Taking the straps off did not free the animal, as Ivan found out.

"Son of a bitch," he thought, scratching his hands, and getting up on the old bridge to have the advantage of looking into the water. Still he could not tell much of what was going on.

Ivan saw where Antony had made a frantic effort to turn back in the middle of the bridge, but the horse had tried to plod on to cross in time.

"Son of a whore – you're smarter than the old man," Ivan said, while large inch-long mooseflies landed on the back of the horse's ears and on the old scars made from the straps. The horse shook his head, and looked around when Ivan spoke to him. Then he sighed one of those plaintive horse sighs, and lowered his head and sucked some water.

"Well – I'm going – I can't be expected to stay here – I've got Sudbury to think of," Ivan said.

Ivan got almost two hundred yards away, and waited. The horse was very small. His head was down, and every now and then he looked over at him calmly, as if to see where he was.

Ivan lit a cigarette and kept batting the flies from his head. He'd grab deerflies out of the air with his right hand and crush them, saying: "How do you like me now, you cocksucker?"

Then he said to the horse: "I'm not going back to you – so you don't have to look in this direction, because I'm on my way to Sudbury – take a piece of ass on the train for once." He then butted his cigarette, though he didn't know why, since the fire Antony had started was burning right towards him.

The horse simply looked his way and when it moved its head its two silver bells jingled. Ivan sighed and scratched his ear. Then, taking his hands and rubbing mud off his new corduroy pants, he walked into the water, and back towards the horse.

Reaching the animal once more, he began packing the horse's hide with mud to keep the flies away from it.

Just then, the top part of the bridge, which was dry as shredded tar paper, caught on fire.

"Ah, you motherfucker," he said, and, taking off his jacket and soaking it in water, he climbed atop the bridge and began beating down the flames, now and then kicking at the rotted planking with his feet.

It was after one in the afternoon. The giant maple

waved in the distance, as flecks of ash-coloured sunlight filtered dazzlingly through its boughs. The first things to catch on fire were the nettles beneath it, which served as a springboard for this whole section of woods. Ivan tried to calm his growing fear and instinctively stuck close to the animal next to him.

✣ ✣ ✣

There were other people who were surprised by the fire. Ruby Madgill was one. She had brushed Tantramar, turned him out, brought him in, and groomed him completely, and then saddled him ready to go for a ride. When she got into the saddle she looked up and saw the smoke.

"Where you going?" Lloyd said.

"I'm riding over to the house," she answered, holding the reins tight so that Tantramar continued to back as Lloyd spoke.

"Well, don't go too far – look at the fire."

"Ah, for Christ's sake," she said.

And she slapped the horse with a crop and he broke into a fast trot, leaning right, out of the paddock.

Ruby was very upset with everyone these last three weeks. She tormented Lloyd. She came in at three in the morning and slept until noon – and the meticulous care of her horse this morning was just a part of the common thread of her dissatisfaction with the summer, her anger at Dorval Gene, and her refusal to look Armand Savard in the eye, when they passed each other on the road in their cars.

Off she rode to see her house. The day was very bright and the sky was glossy blue in the distance.

Ruby had hoped the fire would destroy her new house, but she had no such luck.

"It's likely I'll be living in the fucking thing yet," she said looking at it. "What a cocksuckin monstrosity you are – ninety thousand dollars worth of brick shit-house if you ask me!"

The trouble was she couldn't find the fire at all, and wearing her tight breeches, and high English-style riding boots, she rose and fell on the saddle, hoping that the fire would come out and destroy something so she could see it.

But there were only some puffs of smoke in the distant sky, and the leaves at the edge of the field were turning golden by the late-August nights. There was a smell of fall in the air.

She brought her right foot out of the stirrup and hooked it over the saddle, and taking an orange from her pocket, peeled it with her long fingernails, sucking at it as she did, and, looking towards the trees, rested the crop between her legs.

Now a column of smoke plummeted towards the south, far above her head – and a new, darker smoke billowed inside the greyish cloud.

She looked at it and sniffed the wind, found the stirrup, and holding the reins tight, jabbed the horse softly, so that Tantramar, already glossy with sweat, moved backwards, the sound of its hooves sharp on the stones beneath it.

Ruby kept backing the horse up, until it turned on the right lead and began to canter about the property, its head high because of her contact on the reins, and its black coat as glossy as the saddle beneath her. Because its head was held so high it stepped on loose boards and planks, and cut its right hoof on a chip of cement that had a nail embedded in it.

She kept riding the horse like this, for twenty minutes, hitting it with the crop each time it slowed its pace, and surveying her property. After a while, she brought the horse back to a walk, and looked behind her with her hand on the horse's rump. She saw a tuft of bright green grass just below her bedroom window. "I love you as the grass is green," she remembered Missle Ryan say. "I love you as the grass is green," she said now, to no one, it seemed, but the horse's rump.

Then she went home, and not bothering to unsaddle or cool down the animal, left it in its stall, walked into the house, and sat in Big Clay's cold black-leather chair in the den, with his gun collection in the rack behind her beautiful head, and tears in her eyes.

Cindi had gone with her mother to the station, leaving a note that she would meet Ivan there, and writing that she had taken all the bags, in her scrawl that was unreadable because she had never gotten over the habit that when she crossed a *t*, she crossed out the whole word. So the note was posted on the door, the cupboards opened, and the bathroom light left on.

And there, at the station, she began her wait in her new pantsuit, with the Elizabethan-collared blouse with long white sleeves, holding her gigantic houseplant on her lap, every now and then peering through it when the door opened, and blinking her albino-coloured eyelashes.

Nevin had lost control of himself completely and was terrorizing everyone. He had moved all of the furniture into the middle of the field, and waving a stick and shouting, made the little girls, who were sitting hugging each other, shake like leaves.

Although ten people dropped by to help him, and each one of them said that he shouldn't move the furniture, he was determined to move it. He ordered Vera in to pack her china, and ordered Ralphie to help him carry the cabinet out.

And every time someone obeyed him, he would nod in an aggressive way, as if this was the best feeling he had ever had. Then, about three o'clock, all the furniture that they had piled in the field burned, but with the neighbours helping they managed to save the house.

The black smoke rising in the cloud of grey smoke Ruby had seen was the lumber that had been upset on the old bridge finally going up in flames. Ivan was walking chest deep in water beneath it because of his fresh worry – that the entire bridge, as old and as rickety as it was, was about to fall upon the horse. And Rudolf, sensing this, was looking behind him, and Ivan was trying to find ways to prop the bridge up.

"What we gotta do, Rudolf, is find out a way to haul her in the other direction when she goes – and that might be the fuckin ticket all around."

Then Ivan went beneath the water to get a look at things. The horse's outside hind leg was stretched back and caught up under the runner, and probably broken.

Ivan came up, took a finger and wiped his nose.

"You got yourself in one fuck of a mess here, Rudie," he said. "How did you let the old man talk you into this," he said, as he walked in front of it. Ivan, for the first time, felt feeble in his efforts to do anything, and in his sudden anger he took to beating the horse to make it lunge. "Come on you son of a bitch, come on," he said, "you fuckin cocksucker – move."

The old horse made three or four great lunges, tearing up the mud and roots beneath it, splashing itself up to the blinkers, wheezing and showing its blackened teeth. And after Ivan's fury, settling down seven inches from where it was before, with the bridge on fire just above its head.

"Ah, ya poor broke-up son of a whore," Ivan said, looking at the horse's tarnished studded collar, and its flags and two little bells. "If I had half an I.Q., I'd be on my way to Sudbury."

Stepping away from the horse and shaking his fist, he yelled, "Sudbury, Sudbury, Sudbury – where you can't find me to get you out of fuckin scrapes like this here. Because you are a dumb horse – TROY is a smart horse, and right now he's in his stall eating hay. And where are you? Answer me that!" he said, crying suddenly.

Then he walked furiously across the bog and into the woods, wiping tears from his eyes. He came out a minute later dragging a pole three times as long as he was. He was going to jar the bridge the other way. Once he did that, he felt he would have much better luck moving the sleigh.

The horse wheezed and coughed, and watched him with the pathetic stoic eyes seen so often in beasts of burden; the little flags on its blinkers, crooked, and the coarse twine unravelling from its bobbed tail.

Ivan, tears still in his eyes, laughed when he looked at the flags, and got upon the horse's back to straighten them out.

Then suddenly, out of the blue, the old horse's ears caught on fire as sparks flew in a great billow, snapping at the air.

Ivan, furious at this, put them out with his bare hands, yelling: "I'd rather you die of smoke than flame."

Then he laughed because of the way the ears smoked, and then cried for the same reason.

"You know what I've just been thinking, Rudie," he began to say, "that goddamn Cindi is probably at this moment –"

But just then the bridge unceremoniously tumbled upon them both.

15

By November there was snow on the ground. People could walk on the icy fields through the woods and not see a living sign of an animal, only the eerie, indefinable, and somehow calculated design of ice webs in the burnt-out trees.

One day a little coyote padded out across the field, with a small body but great big paws and ears. It walked into old Allain's yard and stole a chicken.

Antony came out with the .30-.30, fired at it four times, but missed it every time. Then he walked back into the house and sat down.

Then, sticking his tongue into his cheek to puff it out, he got Valerie to kiss him, and without looking at her, hauled his last Extra Big chocolate bar from his pocket.

Then he took a walk to see Vera and Nevin and their new baby girl.

He would come over every day now to talk to them. It didn't matter what he talked about. Sometimes it was the weather – the storm that might come, the planet might explode, something was going on in Lemec with the snow crabs, or he had heard Clay Everette had finally been put in his place at a horse-hauling in Napan – and he would sit there and drink tea.

He said nothing about the past summer. Once in a while when someone mentioned the past summer he would look at them, with casual interest, as if he were a stranger that had just been informed about events that were unknown to him.

He found that it was best not to mention Margaret to them, so he did not. And he sensed that it was true that Nevin was going to go away for a while, and Vera was going to move to town.

The birth of Hadley – for this is what the little girl was called – happened at night. Just as Vera could not have foreseen that she would become pregnant, and then believed it was her moral choice that she had, she did not foresee the events of the birth either. Two weeks before her due date her water had broken when she was visiting Thelma, and so it was convenient to cross the road to the hospital, where the baby was born in the delivery room, and because it was going to be a dry birth and inducing didn't work – they were forced to do a Caesarean.

And this is what Vera spent her time talking about to Antony, believing that she alone was responsible for everything that had happened – and therefore more content than at any time in her life.

Antony didn't talk too much about his own family any more. Sometimes he would mention Valerie's marks on a test at school. And on occasion when someone mentioned Gloria, he would look at them and nod seriously.

He seemed unsure of himself now and didn't do too much outside any more. For instance, he didn't go down river and drink beer. Nor did he go up to Madgill's to get his alimony cheque. It came by mail now – always a little late, and signed by Clay Everette.

They had heard that Tantramar got sick and had to be put down. But the news from the family was that Ruby had gotten married to someone one night at the church in Chatham Head. But he didn't talk about this. It seemed natural, it seemed inevitable, and it seemed pointless.

Antony would return the conversation to the snow crabs in Lemec, or to a weather balloon he saw drifting high in the sky, so high in fact that he thought it was a spaceship – and then look at them with the hope that they would believe him.

He told Vera he could get her another piano, but they didn't seem to believe him – until he arrived at three in the morning with it loaded on a truck. Antony stood in mud up to his knees, with the lights on and the truck motor throttling in the dark, and with a song playing on the radio in the cab, which smelled of pine freshener. He refused to take money for it, telling Nevin it was for his summer's work.

Then he got Jeannie and Frank Russell to help him unload it and carry it into the house. Frank, his red, freckled hands showing in the porch light, and Jeannie standing in behind, with her gum boots to her knees, and her hearing aid turned up full volume.

So there was an atonement of a sort, the red hands under the porch light, and Jeannie's decisive nod to Vera when she entered the house, wearing her husband's long brown coat, walking squat on her thin sturdy legs, her gum boots squeaking, and her hands clutching the rim of the piano like some little Tasmanian devil, while Vera stood in her nightgown and could do nothing more than offer them hot chocolate – for that was the only luxury in the world Vera allowed herself.

Whenever Antony left Vera's, he would go home through the field and out behind his shed. He would walk into the house and up the stairs slowly. Sitting on the edge of his bed, he would stare glumly at the dresser. Then, lying his head on the pillow, with the clock ticking beside him, he would listen as the wind rattled the window and people moved about downstairs.

A year passed before Cindi got married again. Her maid of honour was a girl from Welshford, who was a friend of the groom, so she had moved out of the sphere of people surrounding Ivan's case, moved away from it – and into a new life and mythology, which caused the standard speculations of how it would differ from her previous life.

What was unfortunate, some people said now, was that she would ever get married again. Thelma only sighed. She sighed, because she believed the sigh made her look concerned and understanding. And then she looked at Vera and Olive – who she hoped would approve of her sigh.

The whole idea, especially from Olive, was that if Cindi had only talked to her, or to somebody like "her" (and here she cast a kindly look at Adele who was not, of course, like "her"), then she would not have jumped right into another marriage. The whole idea that she was pregnant again was awful. The idea was again fostered that she was a simpleton, and was taken advantage of – and another idea complemented it – she was a simpleton who took advantage of others – those who last year had tried to help her, and straighten her about.

The only one of them who went to the wedding was Adele. It looked so eerie. Cindi was more than a little pregnant and was already showing. A band played outside the church with a set of bagpipes. Confetti was thrown, and all was the same as before.

Cindi went past Adele without recognizing her. She had gone into another group, another life. The car door was opened and she waved, caught Adele's wave, and blinked in the sunlight.

Adele went into the graveyard, which was sectioned in two.

The section near the bay was the graves of the first settlers, and the graves nearest the woods were the newer ones.

At one of the newest graves Adele stopped. Her lips trembled, and then she shrugged. The granite marker in the earth simply read:

Ivan Basterache
A Man
1957-1979

It was quite a famous marker for a while. And then it was overgrown and forgotten altogether.

Afterword

BY WAYNE JOHNSTON

I met David Adams Richards in 1983 in his first year as writer-in-residence at the University of New Brunswick. I was a graduate student, taking a course in fiction writing from Bill Bauer, who invited him to visit his class. I had heard of Richards before coming to the University of New Brunswick, but I had not read his books. All I knew of him was that some readers said they detected in his work the influence of William Faulkner and compared his fictional Miramichi region with Faulkner's Yoknapatawpha County.

Dave came into class that day carrying a Styrofoam cup, which I presumed contained coffee. In fact, it contained nothing. It would, by slow degrees throughout his reading, fill up with spit from the plug of tobacco he had wedged between his jawbone and his teeth. He paused while he read, and without a trace of self-consciousness or even an inkling that this was not a standard practice among visitors to creative-writing classes, spat and spewed tobacco juice into the cup. I remember looking around the class to see how the others were reacting. No one seemed to want to be the first person to let on that they did not know that this was what readers of fiction did while pausing between paragraphs.

He read from the book of his that is still my favourite, *Lives of Short Duration*. He read mesmerizingly, as I had never heard anyone read before. Those who have heard him know exactly what I mean. It is impossible to describe what it was like to anyone who has not. He read with great conviction, and his unstinting, unqualified love for every one of his characters came through in every line.

It was not then fashionable to love your characters. It still isn't, I suppose. Certainly, it was and is unheard-of to love *all* of them. There was the sense in his voice and in the sentences I was hearing for the first time that he considered everyone to be caught up in the same joyful and ridiculous predicament.

He read the section from *Lives* about Little Simon and Blinkie, who were so often seen together that there was a rhyme about them. Blinkie could not sleep, so bothered was he by the sound of a cricket, which he swore was coming from behind the immovable fridge. To mollify Blinkie, Little Simon went in search of the cricket, even though he couldn't hear it. It was one of the funniest set pieces I had ever heard, so I was mystified as to why almost no one else in the class was laughing. Perhaps they all knew what was coming: Blinkie's death and Little Simon, while in mid-air, clicking his heels, seeing Blinkie on the undertaker's cutting board. As the passage moved from tender comedy to sorrow, the cadence of Dave's voice did not change. The account of Little Simon and Blinkie's happiness and friendship read like an elegy, and in the account of their misfortune and Blinkie's death there was a wonderful, indefinable redemption.

Somewhere in the reading was this sentence: "The snow flurried darkly upon the pavement like some northern apparition." The hairs stood up on the back of my neck. I had seen snow do exactly that, had felt exactly upon seeing it do that as I felt upon hearing Dave Richards read this sentence. Not since I was a child had a sentence in a book erased for me so completely the gap between mind and world, life and literature.

As I would come to realize, there was, as far as Dave is concerned, no such gap. Dave reads books as if they are letters from friends about people he has known forever. Or rather, the books he likes read as if they are letters from friends about people he has known forever. If he does not like a book, it is because he does not think it does what a letter to a friend should do. It does not tell what the letter-writer believes to be the truth.

Dave and I became friends, but not because, or at least not just because, we liked each other's work.

Since meeting Dave, I have discovered that a disconcertingly large number of people not only like but seem to understand the sport of curling. That there are few things more enjoyable than to watch a truly awful movie with someone whose appreciation of cinematic wretchedness is even greater than your own. That if you are invited to the summer cottage of a friend, you may be assigned a bed whose mattress is dented down the middle as if, merely to accommodate you, your host has gone to the considerable pains of removing from it the anvil it contained for twenty years. That a friend should not be taken seriously the first five hundred and seventy-three times he tells you he is moving to Toronto. I have discovered how wrong I was when I was twenty-four and believed that close friendships would be easy to come by.

It is not very often that you can point to a moment in your life and say that there, exactly there, something happened that changed you forever, something after which your life was never quite the same again.

I can think of three or four such times, and meeting Dave Richards that fall night in Bill Bauer's class was one of them.

These, my memories of a close friend and great writer, David Adams Richards, are the best thing I can offer by way of an afterword to this wonderful book, *Evening Snow Will Bring Such Peace*. It was written before it became common knowledge among readers that David Adams Richards was,

229

among many other laudable things, one of this country's funniest writers. His comedy does not consist of slapstick or rely on wordplay. It is the tender comedy of the human heart, a comedy born of the limitless compassion he feels for his characters.

This story of the Basterache family, from the misunderstood-by-all Cindi, whose capacious heart and soul are the heart and soul of the novel, to Ivan, her husband, who is the victim of the most profound betrayal, to Ruby, who is more interested in changing the world – i.e., Cindi – than she is in changing herself, is written unashamedly against the grain of postmodernism. These are characters who love and hate each other and whom the writer wants readers to view no differently than they would people they meet in real life.

To David Adams Richards, the point of literature is to lead both his characters and readers to a redemption that is no less joyful for being difficult to attain. *Evening Snow Will Bring Such Peace* will bring, to the open-hearted, open-minded reader, the sense of peace promised by its magnificent title. The "peace which passeth understanding."

The New Canadian Library
The Best of Canadian Writing

Titles by David Adams Richards

The Coming of Winter
Afterword by Rick Hillis

David Adams Richards's first novel, written when he was twenty-two, *The Coming of Winter* reveals an author who finds universal truths in the particular rural setting of New Brunswick's Miramichi Valley. An intensely realistic story with engaging, unaffected characters, the novel provides a window on a world as unsettling, as uncontrollable, and as inescapably authentic as a sudden brawl.

Blood Ties
Afterword by Merna Summers

Blood Ties. For David Adams Richards the expression is an assertion of the reality of life in small-town Canada, where blood ties people in countless, almost unknowable ways to friends, community, and landscape. Using dazzling angles of vision and shifting perspectives, Richards captures the lives of his characters with sympathy and understanding.

Lives of Short Duration
Afterword by Alistair MacLeod

The Terris are engaging people, but they are a family in collapse. In their petty and wasted state, they typify aspects of the larger community, besieged by financial woes and creeping economic and cultural Americanization. Yet while the novel's characters are at times vicious, sleazy, and even outright dim, Richards entitles them to the interest and sympathy of the reader.

—— *NCL* *A series worth collecting* ——

Nights Below Station Street
Afterword by P.K. Page

Nights Below Station Street, a haunting chronicle set in a small northern New Brunswick mill town, centres on the Walsh family: Joe, optimistic in the face of continuing unemployment; his wife, Rita, willing to believe the best about people; and their teenage daughter Adele, whose explosive but caring relationship with her father wars constantly with her desire for independence. Richards uses his remarkable powers of observation and sympathy to delineate his characters' wayward emotions and their inner lives.

Evening Snow Will Bring Such Peace
Afterword by Wayne Johnston

Ivan and Cindi Basterache have been married only twenty months, but rumours of violence begin to spread throughout the town. Their subsequent separation throws into relief the frustrated lives of the people around them, whose concern and interventions reveal the sometimes cruel truths that lie at the root of good intentions. Brutal yet tender-hearted, *Evening Snow Will Bring Such Peace* explores the strange power we all share to shape one another's destinies.

For Those Who Hunt the Wounded Down
Afterword by Joan Clark

In a small northern New Brunswick mill town Jerry Bines, acquitted of murder, returns home to his estranged wife and young son. But when he learns that Gary Percy Rils has escaped from prison, he fears for his own safety and that of others. Bines's attempt to protect his family from Rils leads inevitably to the novel's harrowing climax.